NOTES FROM APPRECIATI

A rare story that comes around only once in a while. A poignant and humorous tale of family, friends and finance that instructs and uplifts the reader, young and adult. It will stay relevant to your life for weeks, months, and even years after you read it.
    Courtney Burnett,
    Early Childhood Educator, M.Ed., BCBA

A book of fabulously written imagery - with virtue. (Much stronger than Avatar, and that was in 3-D!)
    Sharon K. Griffin,
    Retired Director AES, Univ. of WA.

This story is stunningly written with imagination and wit. It is an enduring tale.
    Karen McMillan,
    Educator, M Ed., BFA

A delightful multi-layered story for all ages, and a good book to use for character education. My students and I loved it. It is now one of my yearly "read-alouds."
    Jolie Aronson,
    MS, fourth/fifth grade teacher. Walmart and Sam's Club Teacher of the year 2007, Grays Harbor, Pacific County, WA

Entering the world of Marmalada Mouse, her attic friends and downstairs family is, in a word, heartwarming. I plan to slip between the covers and revisit those folks often.
    Elaine L. Burnett,
    Hostess Exemplar

Written with charming insight and whimsy. Marmalada Mouse and her acquaintances are remindful of Beatrix Potter's country creatures, and suggest more tales to follow.
    Karen Greenhill Edwards,
    Reading Specialist

A hilarious, fun read and a most creative use of our language. Just plain charming!
    Forest P. Watson,
    Entrepreneur

The thing that sticks in my mind is the author's ability to paint pictures with words.
> *Susan Barrow,*
> *Interior Decorator/Organizer*

Gayolin Bailey is an amazing writer. Talented, insightful, creative. In this whimsical tale her unusual characters come alive and challenge us to examine the way we are constructing our own lives.
> *Denny Rydberg,*
> *President, Young Life*

Why, this is simply the best book I ever read! If it doesn't receive widespread recognition and acclamation, then something is surely wrong in the literary world!
> *Ilene Olsby,*
> *Centenarian.*
> *Mother of the author.*

UPSTAIRS DOWNSTAIRS

A Tale of Two Stories

Copyright © 2010

All rights reserved. No part of this book may be used or reproduced in any manner whatsoever without written permission from the publisher.

Cover Design, Photography and Graphics
by the amazing
Bruce Barton Bailey

To Hilary and Camille, heroes both,
and to those wonderful people
who call me Gramma:

Addison Rain
Avery Campbell
Axel James
Bam Anthony
Courtney Rose
Jesse Alexander
Kent Charles
Merrick Michael
Nigel Orion
Olivia Zajda
Shalon Louise
Sienna Meadow
Tiffany Lee

A NOTE TO THE GROWN UP READER

In our early thirties, my husband, Bruce, and I socialized loosely among business friends who put on fabulously uppity cocktail parties. Tables were laden with pyramids of prawn surrounded by foie gras, caviar and cheeses of every odor. Wines were sniffed and swirled and slurped, and on occasion poured down the sink in lofty dismay. Guests made stage entrances in full-length mink coats that were casually dropped and abandoned upon arrival.

I had to feel my way around these gatherings to find out if and where I fit because I had grown up eating ordinary liverwurst, Vienna sausage and Spam. My clothes were secondhand, although I was very good at putting them together. And in my upbringing alcoholic beverages were verboten, so I had no idea of the nuances and varieties of wine, nor did I know how to pronounce their names. Once, in a grocery store, I picked up a bottle and asked another customer, "Have you tried this" - I will spell it as I pronounced it - "Mer lot?"

It was because of my husband that we were included at these occasions. The acquaintances were his. And he was, and still is, handsome, smart, quick witted, good on his feet, and funny.

I will never forget standing in a shoulder-to-shoulder crowd in the foyer of a house when a guest gingerly opened the door to come in. She was carrying her toy poodle. Bruce moved out of the way to let her pass by, but promptly insulted both her and her dog. I gasped. She laughed. And several times that evening she found him and tapped him on the shoulder hoping for another insult. He didn't fail to deliver and she laughed every time.

There was another evening when he had a young woman in the grip of his humor, and I happened to come around the corner just as he said something that dropped her helplessly to her knees. Although she and I didn't converse that night, as it turned out, she had taken notice of me anyway. And she asked f the friends we had come with, "Who's the mouse Bruce Bailey's married to?"

I tried to get my feelings hurt over that, but I just couldn't work them up. And a few days later when I spotted a beige ceramic mouse in a gift shop, I bought her and took her home to my kitchen window sill. I liked looking at her.

Well, I can't tell you now what happened to that knickknack mouse, whether she got broken or if I gave or threw her away. But, she is long gone, relegated decades ago to the attic of my mind.

And yet, I don't think she has lain dormant there. I think she has been nosing around my brain for years searching for small treasure like a pig rooting for truffles. And she has finally punched her way back to my consciousness and, actually, even back into my house, sporting a new persona, and insisting that she has something to say. And I must admit I have tried to get in her way because I am afraid. Her voice is so small.

But I can't stand her nagging anymore. So, please, if I may, I would like to introduce Marmalada Mouse to you. And you to her.

G.D.B.

A NOTE TO THE JUNIOR READER

I know something about you that you might not know. Though you are small upon a big earth, like an atom, you are packed with power. You are an ascending star. You are the bright future.

By contrast, since I am old and way past the midpoint of my life, I am falling out of the sky, my flame diminished to flickering embers. Nevertheless, I am not to be counted out quite yet because even in embers there lingers for a while a few tiny hot-red, red hot coals. And they, like matches - as small as they may be - are mighty. With a touch they can burn a forest down or heat a house in winter.

In this story, you will meet Marmalada Mouse and her friends. They are small, too, not only in size, but also in significance because at some time each of them has been discarded. I came upon them in second-hand stores and one by one I bought them and brought them home. Then, as I repaired, painted, dressed, and accessorized them, making them my own, they began to tell me who they are and what they want to say to you.

Now, none of them is beautiful or handsome, so I hope you won't turn away from their homeliness. And each is odd in his or her own way, so you will have to be tolerant.

And, in case your expectations are high, I need to let you know right away that they do not encounter the alchemy of wizards, the ferocity of werewolves or the phantasmagoria of alien worlds.

No, theirs is a small everyday story. And it is my job to write it. And if, perchance, there resides any power in its pages, it will be your job to unpack it.

G.D.B.

UPSTAIRS DOWNSTAIRS

A Tale of Two Stories

The Teakettle chugged a steady blast of steam and whistled a loud and incessant warning.

Mrs. Burjanavetti wheeled around to release the spout cover and rotate the burner control knob back to its lowest setting. She held the kettle to the burner before picking it up, gripping the handle firmly. "I hear you. I hear you," she said sternly, as if she were reprimanding a whining child.

She routinely kept the kettle hot all day, a habit held over from the years when her house was a center of activity and she could count on company dropping by almost every day. It hadn't been that way for some time, however, because her children were grown, she had lost her husband, Max, and many neighborhood friends had moved on. Nevertheless, Mrs. Burjanavetti maintained her ritual of readiness. So after pouring hot water into a waiting cup, she put the kettle back on the burner and returned to the task at hand.

Steadying herself against the island in the center of the kitchen, she tipped a pan off the rack above her head, wincing as it settled into her grip. "How did you get so heavy?" she asked, letting it thump against the cutting-block. She rubbed her wrist for a moment and then, ignoring the ache in her arm, went to work making "Cowboy Stew," an oddly-named vegetarian meal she had improvised one evening with minimal groceries on hand.

Mrs. Burjanavetti smiled every time she put this "stew" together, remembering the first time she had made it. Her children were young at the time and her husband, underemployed, so making meals for a family of four from semi-bare cupboards was the norm for a few years. And sometimes that made her mad.

Alone in the kitchen that afternoon, she flung cupboard doors open and slammed them shut. In rebellion to her situation she let the refrigerator door stand open and the kitchen faucet run unnecessarily. And she threw ingredients carelessly into the sauce pan, and utensils into the sink.

But anger had not negated her magical culinary touch. At dinner that night, after getting everything that could be pierced by a fork, her husband swiped his plate several times with his index finger to get the very last bit of sauce. He looked up at her guiltily with his finger in his mouth, expecting her to comment on his lack of table manners, but she was holding back a smile. His hand fell hard on the table and he addressed her sternly, using her given name, Frances, instead of his pet name for her, Kiddo. "Have you started writing that cookbook yet?" he asked impatiently.

And then with a sloppy wave of his arm he sent nine year old Emerlin to get paper and pencil from his desk and told her to be secretary while Mrs. B dictated what she had done in the kitchen. Mrs. B understood his gruff and indirect way of complimenting her, so she happily obliged. Writing a cookbook had been his idea for her and not hers for herself, however, and it wasn't something she was interested in doing. But for the moment, she left that unsaid.

When it came time to put a title at the top of the page, the conversation turned into an argument between Emerlin and her seven year old brother, Sterling, who wore a holster at all times, even when he went to bed. So it took a draw of toothpicks to decide who the "namer" would be. Sterling won. And no amount of persuasion could convince him that cowboys and vegetables didn't pair up very well or that what they had just eaten was not by definition a stew.

Sterling never outgrew his fascination with all things Western and when he was in his early twenties, he left Washington State and moved to Montana where he became a rancher. His college sweetheart, Angela, followed him there, and they settled down in Hamilton, a town nestled between the Bitter Root and Sapphire Mountains.

But Emerlin stayed in the Seattle area, and visited her mother regularly with her husband, Big Guy, and their children, Jimmy and Lissa. And Cowboy Stew was in the making for them.

Leaving sauce to simmer and bread dough to rise, Mrs. Burjanavetti fussed over the dining room table.

She opted for a white table cloth instead of placemats and cotton napkins rather than paper. She snipped herbs from the back yard - rosemary, mint, lavender, and oregano - and arranged them into jam-jar bouquets for every place setting except Jimmy's. He got dandelion, a flower they both agreed was under appreciated.

When she closed the drapes and slid the dimmer switch up and down to find the right balance between mood and visibility, she noticed a few stubborn stains in the table covering that hadn't come out in the last wash. So she added a random array of votive candles to the tabletop, artistically hiding the unwelcome marks. "New job description for you," she said, addressing the tablecloth with a rap of her knuckles. "After tonight you're a drop cloth."

Mrs. Burjanavetti put her plate next to Jimmy's because it was his turn to sit next to her. She kept track of such details both out of a grandmotherly compulsion to make things equal between the children and a desire to head off bickering. Emerlin and Big Guy would sit at the ends of the table, as usual, Big Guy in the chair with arms, the one that had been Mr. Burjanavetti's.

Big Guy was an easy person to remember after a first introduction. He was tall, had a commanding voice that went with his stature, and his given name and family name were the same. He was James Alexander James. However, when he first began dating Emerlin, her father deliberately disremembered his name for a while, just as he had done with all of the other young men who had shown an interest in his daughter. Several times he greeted James with "Hey, how ya doin' there, big guy," swinging his arm out wide to the side and back in again, hard, making a collision out of a handshake.

James shrugged off the intended intimidation, however, and after a few visits took liberties himself with their family name. "I'm doin' fine, Mr. B. How 'bout you?" Both nicknames stuck. James became Big Guy, and the Burjanavettis, Mr. and Mrs. B. Eventually Mrs. B became "Mom."

"Hey, we're lookin' pretty fancy tonight," Big Guy said as they gathered around the table.

Mrs. B curtsied in response to his compliment, and after all the special details had been duly noted, she gathered up the dinner plates and took them to the kitchen. When she brought them back, everyone hummed approval at the sight of red-potato scramble generously covered with a creamy cheese sauce studded with capers, crisp greens and tomato wedges drizzled with oil and lemon vinaigrette, and hunks of hot buttered French bread still sizzling from the broiler.

After everyone's dinner was down, Mrs. B walked around the table with freshly grated Parmesan cheese. Scooping it up in her fingers, she went from person to person and dribbled a generous portion onto each plate as reverently as if she were conducting a baptism.

When Big Guy pulled Mrs. B's chair for her, Lissa impatiently asked that somebody hurry and say the blessing. Jimmy volunteered. "God is great. God is good. And we thank God for our fuhd. Amen."

Mrs. B, unsure of her ears, curled her hand around his skinny arm and asked, "What was that last word?"

Jimmy flipped his straight brown hair away from his eyes with a jerk of his head. "I said amen, Gramma. It was the end of the prayer."

"No, no, no. The word before amen," Mrs. B warned. "And you know that's what I meant." She gave his arm a half-mean squeeze.

"Oh, you mean fuhd?" Jimmy pretended surprise. "Well, that prayer is a poem, Gramma, and poems are supposed to rhyme.

I could have said 'God is great, God is gude, and we thank God for our food,' but I like the first one better."

Mrs. B let go of his arm and relaxed into the back of her chair. "You know, Jimmy," she said, "Poems don't have to rhyme that exactly. Some poets employ a technique called slant rhyme …"

"I'm gonna' want seconds," he said, cutting off her badly timed literary tidbits.

"How can you know that?" she asked. "You haven't even started eating yet."

Jimmy dug into his dinner gracelessly, jutting his head low over his plate and gripping his fork with a fist. "Don't be surprised, Gramma, if I even want thirds," he said with his mouth full. But, trying as he did, he couldn't keep up with himself. So he announced that he would take his second helping later on that evening. "There's no rule that says you have to eat them right away," he asserted, ready to defend his brand new and very literal definition of seconds and thirds. Mrs. B decided not to spar with him.

Mrs. B shooed everyone to the living room when it came time to do the dishes.

Emerlin followed her back to the kitchen, however, where they acted out their after-dinner ritual - Mrs. B refusing her daughter's help while donning an apron and Emerlin ignoring her mother's protestations while tucking a kitchen towel into the waistband of her jeans.

Mrs. B watched Emerlin. She was always struck by her prettiness and would have liked to think that her daughter was a younger version of herself. But she had never been slender like Emerlin, nor was she as tall, nor were her features quite as refined. After tightening the bow of her apron, Mrs. B tipped her head back and gave her hair a vigorous fluffing, reminding herself of her greatest physical attribute. Naturally curly, her brown hair had turned silver. And sometimes, when sunlight caught its sheen just right, an observer might think she had a verifiable aura. It wasn't unusual for people to comment on it, and she was as likely to agree with them and solicit further compliments as she was to simply say thank you.

Mrs. B filled the sink with hot soapy water to take care of the items she didn't like to put into the dishwasher, which included almost everything. She worked inefficiently, letting her hands idle in the hot suds when important points of conversation were being exchanged. It took them an hour to finish. And then, after Emerlin had finally hung the last pan back on its hook and wiped down the countertops, it didn't occur to either one of them to sit down and chat in comfort. They stood at the sink, leaning against the damp counter, shifting weight from foot to foot, sharing their views on world events and God and diets and interior decorating, things they talked about repeatedly, yet never with any sense of boredom.

'What's goin' on out there?" Big Guy yelled from the couch. "I'm lonesome."

"We just now finished," Mrs. B called back, grimacing guiltily as Emerlin rattled the silverware drawer for sound effect. "And, I was about to make some decaf to go with the ice cream you brought. Want some?"

"Love it," he said gratefully. "Tell me when it's ready. I'll come out there."

They ate dessert in the kitchen. Mrs. B and Emerlin sat in the nook, the children jumped up on the counters and Big Guy stood, leaning against the stove. "Mom," he said, pushing the spoon around in his bowl. "Any way you can see yourself clear for one more loan? Just twenty-five hundred like last time. And only for three months. That's when we finally get our share of the buyout and I just need to cover a couple of payments until then. After that, we're out of the woods."

Big Guy took a deep breath and slowly carved out a chunk of ice cream. He was weary from working a job he didn't like, but one he hadn't dared quit until he and Emerlin recovered financially from a failed business venture. Asking Mrs. B for money from her moderate savings embarrassed Big Guy. He wished Mr. B were still there to throw his hands in the air in mock disbelief and lecture him with exaggerated disapproval. Big Guy could work up a good mad then at somebody besides himself. "Mom," he said, looking at her. "I promise I'll do whatever it takes to make sure that Emerlin gets a house she can call her own."

Whatever mistakes had been made, Mrs. B reminded herself that Big Guy was a good man. She looked back at him, her eyes squinting with sincerity as she attempted to convey as much trust as she could muster. "I know you will," she said.

They pursued the subject of finances which unsettled Lissa and Jimmy because their parents argued about money. But to their relief, the conversation took a silly turn. Mrs. B got excited about what she thought would be timely budgetary advice - counsel she had imparted to Big Guy and Emerlin in her daydreams a number of times, and it had always elicited their profuse, albeit imaginary, gratitude and respect.

Because she had ice cream in her mouth, however, Mrs. B waved her spoon in the air to hold the floor until she was able to swallow. But she made the ice cream last longer than necessary, taking an extra moment to formulate the best approach. She decided to avoid the words "you should." Instead, she would put her idea out there gingerly, couching it in a humble shuffle about how she was probably proposing something they already knew.

But, Mrs. B hadn't counted on the cold numbing her tongue, and when the word "perhaps" fell out of her mouth as "puhapth," she knew she'd never get past that first word. And as could have been predicted, "puhapth" came back at her immediately in a sarcastic echo from Big Guy and Emerlin simultaneously. And Big Guy didn't let it end there. "Could I have thecondth on the ithe cream, puhapth?" he asked. Hilarity ruled the rest of a conversation that was peppered with contrived mispronunciations. Lissa and Jimmy joined in, relishing the fun along with the dessert.

Big Guy and Emerlin took their coffee to the living room and turned on the television. Mrs. B took hers to the basement, joining the children for a promised hour in the furnace room where they sat around an abused card table busying themselves on art projects. They worked in silence except for occasional interjections of "Look, Gramma. See what I did?" and "Mm-mm, I do see. That's very good."

Jimmy taped a gel pen drawing to the wall and surveyed the dingy room around him, a space dominated by an old octopus style furnace. He noted its hot arms branching along the low ceiling and looked forward to the first accidental burn on the top of his head that would tell him he was approaching his father's height. He studied the cement-block walls, dirtied by soot. They were gallery walls to him, displaying a dozen pages torn from his spiral binder. Rickety plywood shelves listed into a corner, stressed by the weight of creative resource material, free for his taking.

"This is the best room in your whole house, Gramma," he said. "I wish we had one in ours." He spoke as if he were wishing for the impossible.

"Well, why don't you make that happen, Jimmy," Mrs. B was quick to say. "My shelves over there would probably breathe a sigh of relief if you took some of that stuff off them." It was then that she glanced at her watch and saw that not one, but almost two hours had gone by. "Oh, my, you'll have to do that in the morning," she said. "Five more minutes, and then it's time for bed."

Mrs. B wrapped up the evening.

She took the teapot off the stove, refurbished the tea tray and readied the percolator for morning coffee. Then she turned off the television, draped a comforter over Big Guy and Emerlin who had fallen asleep spoon-style on the sofa, and supervised the brushing of teeth before putting the children to bed.

"Gramma," Lissa said, as Mrs. B tucked her in tightly. "Remember when you were a teenager and you were getting off the bus and you, like, turned around to smile at some boys and then you fell out the door onto the parking strip? Will you tell us that story again?"

"Oh, yeah," blurted Jimmy, abruptly sitting up and undoing his covers. "And I want to hear the one about when you went to the party and you had dog-do on the top of your shoe!" (Anything that exited a body, whether solid, liquid, or gas, held particular fascination for Jimmy, so his request was predictable.)

Mrs. B turned out the bedroom light and told her stories again, delighting the children one more time with tales of her childhood embarrassments, humiliations that time had kindly converted into a comedic offering.

Lissa's attention strayed as Mrs. B generously launched into a third story. "Gramma?" she asked solemnly. "Do you know what happened to me last week?"

Mrs. B tolerated the interruption easily. "No, I don't," she said. "You'll have to tell me."

"There's these girls at school?" Lissa continued, speaking as usual in a series of question-like sentences that would ultimately lead to a final declarative statement. "And every day they, like, tease me, and say bad stuff to me?"

Heartache gripped Mrs. B. "What do they say, honey?" she asked with a tight throat.

"Well, this girl named Jennifer? She, like, came up really close to my face and she called me a kinky-haired fattie?"

Anger surged through Mrs. B and she found herself wanting to hurt someone else's grandchild.

"And I got so mad," Lissa continued, "that I hit her really hard and she, like, fell down?"

Mrs. B stifled her urge to say "good for you" because she had often cautioned against using violence as a means of solving problems. But she said it in her heart. After all, every rule has its exceptions, and a sound thumping might be just what this Jennifer person needed.

"But," Lissa continued, picking up the pace. "She had a hold of my sleeve and I, like, didn't know it and I fell down on top of her? And for some reason, Gramma, I don't know why, but we both started, like, laughing and laughing? And now you know what? She's my new best friend!"

Taken aback, Mrs. B cleared her throat unnecessarily, using the moment to shift emotional gears before responding. "I'm glad you have a new friend," she said, backing out of the room. "I'll look forward to meeting her. Now, let's go to sleep on that happy ending, you two," she whispered.

Mrs. B showered quickly without washing her hair and left her towel and clothes in a pile on her bathroom floor. She slipped into silk pajamas, buttoned the top two buttons and dashed for bed. Her head hit the pillow and released a whiff of bleach into the air. Pulling the comforter up around her shoulders and curling up on her side, Mrs. B exhaled a long sigh of gratitude. "Thank you for clean sheets," she said, as if God had done the laundry for her and made up the bed.

Big Guy was the first one up the next morning so he made breakfast.

Mrs. B woke to the aroma of percolating coffee. She remembered telling Jimmy to take some craft materials home with him, and decided that this was a good time to start a general paring down. (The joke in the family was that she regularly "pared up" because she took everything to the attic, lacking the patience for garage sales or for charitable organizations that didn't make pick-ups on her timetable.)

Energized by her new commitment, Mrs. B brushed her teeth, ran a brush through her hair and hurried through her morning meditation. Then she put on her robe and slippers and shuffled to the narrow stairs that led to the attic, an unfinished space that somehow through all the years never did get turned into bedrooms, even though a sub-floor had been laid and two dormers added. It had become, instead, a repository of family history stored in orderly rows of stacked and carefully labeled cardboard boxes. Large items and furniture were backed up against the walls. Mrs. B remembered where most things were so it took little time to retrieve a tarnished silver tea set for Emerlin and an old brass desk lamp for Big Guy.

Her family left happily that morning with craft supplies from the basement, treasures from the attic, leftovers from the refrigerator and a check for twenty-five hundred dollars. Saying goodbye from the end of the driveway, Mrs. B waved as the car accelerated into the street. Jimmy and Lissa, as always, turned backwards and waved goodbye from the rear window until they couldn't see her anymore. That was a rule they had made for themselves and Mrs. B felt responsible to respect their tradition by remaining in their line of sight as long as possible. She waved until the departing car crested an incline in the road and disappeared down the other side.

She lingered there for a while in the comfort and quiet of a warm spring morning. Turning toward the house to feel the sun on her back, Mrs. B found herself facing a neglected front yard. Her husband had always claimed the landscape as his domain. He maintained it authoritatively, planting and transplanting often, tamping the soil with a heavy foot, tying up branches to redirect growth and pruning liberally without hesitation, all of which resulted in a garden that was a bit more tidy than lovely. But after he died, Mrs. B left the yard to itself. There were too many other things to think about.

"Look at you!" she exclaimed. Towering pine and Douglas fir dwarfed the house. Ivy had scaled the chimney and fastened onto a mossy roof. Following the eaves, it trailed Christmas lights that came on at dark all year round. A brown mat of fallen needles had replaced any lawn and a heavy accumulation of dry fronds lay at the base of the dagger ferns. Rhododendron, laden in trusses of crimson and cream, encroached upon the deep purple lilac that managed to finger its way to the light anyway. Its fragrant clusters swayed carelessly in the breeze, too high to reach. Mrs. B felt a pang of neglect, but quickly dismissed it.

Just then, her attention turned to the sound of an approaching figure, a gentleman about her age, handsome in her opinion, who passed by her house almost everyday when the weather was mild. He wore huaraches, and their interwoven leather strips squeaked with every step. Several times he and Mrs. B had exchanged neighborly pleasantries, but she kept them brief because she found herself doubting her appearance at each encounter. Mrs. B acknowledged him this time with just a quick nod and then bent over to pick up the morning paper. She wished she hadn't. Now conscious of her backside, she squeezed her buns tightly when she stood up and minced back to the house, her slippers slapping against her heels as she hurried to the door.

Mrs. B had intended to clear the breakfast table right away, but decided to leaf through the newspaper first. She turned into the living room, stopping to look into the mirror that hung above the sideboard. Studying her image straight on and then slightly to the left and the right, she decided that in spite of the years in her face she looked pretty good for her age and could have afforded to be more cordial that morning, even in her robe and slippers.

She sat on the couch and propped her feet on the coffee table with the paper on her lap. But she fell asleep without reading a word and napped for an hour. When she woke and looked around, it struck her that the trees kept the sun from brightening the room like it used to - she needed to lighten the walls. Delaying the dishes once again, she went to the basement where she pried lids from three cans of previously opened paint. Combining their contents, she blended two whites with a yellow ocher. Then she went back upstairs, secured her robe with a safety-pin, rolled up the sleeves and then rolled on the paint.

Mrs. B talked to the walls while she painted, apologizing for the times when discord had ricocheted throughout the house. She told them to hold on to the laughter and the singing because everything else had long since been forgiven. She rolled on a second coat hoping to seal in the good, and she was sure they understood because that night when she was there alone, still in her robe, sipping tea in the recliner chair, a quiet liveliness pervaded the room, as if some secret garden was on the verge of bloom. It was a sense of presence she could not define and she was content to simply enjoy the comfort of it.

There is a way in which the word "alone" might have to be redefined, however.

A certain little mouse, Marmalada Mouse by name, and a mouse of Mrs. B's very own making, happened to be in the house, too. While Mrs. B busied herself in the living room that day, Marmalada Mouse was busy in the kitchen pilfering items from the cupboards and off the breakfast dishes. She was supposed to be in the attic, having been taken there years before with other store-aways who, like her, had outlived their utility and/or charm.

Marmalada Mouse was a curious breed, having been crafted from an odd assemblage of materials. A spray of wire filament whiskers sprouted next to her nose. Ebony beads were set as pupils in her eyes. Her black long-sleeved blouse topped a skirt of colorful swirls that hung just short of sturdy black hand-me-down shoes, footwear that had once belonged to a store-bought doll. A velveteen jewelry bag, looped over her arm like a tote, completed her ensemble.

Marmalada Mouse had quite a sense of who she was and what she could do. Her eyes, picking up the light no matter which way she turned, her ears poised in alert position, her antenna-like whiskers, her over-sized bag, her sturdy shoes, and her multi-colored skirt which she considered to work as camouflage in interior settings - all of these things together convinced her that she was built for sleuthing. So Mrs. B had been rather naïve to think that a cardboard carton could permanently contain her. And it hadn't. Marmalada Mouse managed to wriggle free from that most unpleasant ensquishment experience almost immediately, suffering a few wrinkles that eventually shook out, and some damage to her ears, frays and tears which she thereafter referred to as piercings. That's when she started wearing earrings.

Banishment to the attic had reunited Marmalada Mouse with old acquaintances who welcomed her warmly to the upstairs with a newcomer's stake of three coins from the big tipped-over penny jar, a tour of her new neighborhood, and a barrage of questions about their long-lost downstairs. She took to attic life easily and often was as busy at night as she was during the day. With shoulders up, neck forward, eyes asquint and the toes of her sturdy shoes tappa-tappa-tapping against the floor, she explored everywhere.

And one night, while skittering along the perimeter of the attic, Marmalada Mouse discovered that the sub-floor ran short of a corner, leaving a small triangular opening that allowed entry into the space between the attic floor and the downstairs ceiling as well as the spaces between the inside and outside walls of the house. Intrigued by such betwixity, Marmalada Mouse lowered herself into its unfamiliar territory, feeling her way along until her eyes became accustomed to darkness. Batting away cobwebs, she slipped in and out of cracks, shinnied studs, followed wires and squeezed between wallboard and insulation. But Marmalada Mouse decided that the maze she had put herself into had no destination, so she decided to go back to the attic.

And just when she was about to turn around, she heard a whoosh, a familiar noise from her days downstairs. Inching in its direction, she came upon a plastic pipe shuddering from the force of water rushing through it and she knew at once that the dishwasher was draining. So without hesitation she jumped down to the pipe and squeezed through the hole in the wall that led to the cupboard beneath the kitchen sink. Although she hadn't set out to do so, Marmalada Mouse had found her way back to downstairs. When she dropped to the cabinet floor she felt the cushion of a sponge beneath her feet and decided to curl up there until morning. That's when her new life would begin, a life that would straddle two worlds - upstairs and down.

From that time on, Marmalada Mouse regularly listened in on downstairs conversations. She watched walls change color, furniture get rearranged, and accent pillows and decorations vary with the seasons. Rooms and closets, drawers and shelves, Marmalada Mouse went everywhere. Once she even rummaged through Mrs. B's jewelry box, climbing right into it and nosing around until she happened upon a small silver ring, an intriguing bijou set with amethyst. It was too big for her fingers, of course, and even for her wrist, but she couldn't get its purple dazzle out of her eyes. So, she toyed with it. And in a moment of silliness, which she thereafter described as inspiration, she plunked it on her head. Well, it fit perfectly as a tiara. So, Marmalada Mouse didn't hesitate to borrow it.

With all the things there were to see, however, her favorite objects of observation were always the children. Unlike her and her attic friends, they didn't stay the same size all their lives or even keep the faces they started out with. Somehow they transformed while still remaining themselves, growing tall like trees and opening up like flowers. And Marmalada Mouse was captivated by such mystery.

So when Lissa and Jimmy came to visit, she abandoned whatever else there was to do in order to watch them eat and run and fight with pillows and play and bathe. She hid herself during the day, but when they fell asleep, she dared to climb onto their downy beds and sniffle at their tousled heads and press her whiskered cheeks against their fingers. She peered into their faces hoping to catch a flash of transformation. And that anticipation settled her down. Content in the still and dim, Marmalada Mouse would watch them as they slept, breathing the rhythm of their breath.

And as long as Jimmy and Lissa were at Mrs. B's house, Marmalada Mouse stayed downstairs as if she had no attic life at all. But when they left, she bounded back up the wall where her friends were waiting, anxious to hear her breathless reports of all that the children had done. She was thankful that they did not feel neglected and that they liked to listen because, as everyone knows, some joys just aren't complete until you have someone to tell them to.

Attic life was simple.

The little store-away people homesteaded in corners and crannies and on two-by-four ledges, bedding down on pillow feathers and packing shreds. They coined street names from the boxes Mrs. B had labeled, such as Family Photos Road, Kitchen Ware Drive, Linens Lane, and Paperbacks Cul de Sac. And there were a few streets called Miscellaneous. A wide center aisle had become their primary meeting place and they called it The Big Broad Way.

Mrs. B interfered with life up there less and less as time had gone by, sometimes only twice a year when she moved the Christmas decorations down and brought them back. So the attic people traveled the crisscross of floor between cardboard cartons with ease, appreciating the safety of their predictable and orderly existence.

But there was one surprising night when the hatch flew open and a rumbling ruckus threatened to disrupt their quiet world. Huddling together, they closed their eyes and hid their faces behind their hands, hoping to hide from a fee-faw-fum that huffed and puffed and scraped and creaked across the room.

When the noise subsided, the attic people peeked through their fingers, and saw to their chagrin that the would-be intruder was only Mrs. B. It was she who had created the racket by dragging a corner cupboard across the attic. Her visit was short. Turning to go, she nervously whisked cobwebs and possible spiders from her hair and clothes and picked up the flashlight she had placed on the floor. Then descending the stairs, she lowered the hatch with each step until it closed. Swiping their foreheads in relief and whispering a collective "whew," most of the attic people agreed that almost having an adventure was all the excitement they would ever need.

Then assuming that attic life would continue its ordinary course, they snuggled back down in their beds and slept. All but Marmalada Mouse. She couldn't close her eyes. Restless, she fluffed and rustled and lay down and sat up and stared at that cupboard, five three-cornered shelves barely visible in the glim of night. "That cupboard just might be ..." was her unfinished thought as she finally fell to sleep, snoring along with the others, none of them suspecting how their lives would begin to change the very next day.

The morning sun cut a swath of light across the attic floor.

People roused, went about their morning routines and then gathered on The Big Broad Way for lunch and a meeting. But Marmalada Mouse had awakened with an idea and she was too preoccupied to eat. She wound the public music box and swayed to music while the others sat, running her hand across the nape of her neck as if to free hair caught in a collar. (Marmalada Mouse didn't actually have hair, but sometimes when she was especially full of herself, she forgot who she was in the mirror and fancied herself the lovely being of her fairy tale imagination.)

Then Marmalada Mouse announced, "A plain little corner isn't enough for me anymore." She placed her hands over her heart and sighed plaintively, "I want decorations and paintings and bouquets and furniture arrangements."

"Sounds highfalutin to me," interjected Sister Mim, wrapping her shawl tightly as if to protect herself from some sort of contamination. She considered Marmalada Mouse to be a bit of a twit, flouncing around in her gaudy outfit, bouncing needlessly from floor to floor and repeating downstairs words such as hasten and behoove.

Sister Mim was a pale figurine who didn't approve of frivolous things so she didn't dance or eat salt or wear lace on her collar. She was white from her hair to her toes, including all of her clothes, making her the only mono-colored person in the whole attic. And that fact bothered her, although she would never say so out loud, and hardly even to herself. And the fact that it bothered her bothered her even more because such discontent contradicted her very own point of view. But she kept all of her botheration a secret and struggled privately to come to terms with her solitary hue.

Nevertheless, a resurging desire not to be odd dogged her, nipping at the edges of her brain, maneuvering her thoughts into flights of wishful fantasy. She wondered if magic wands really worked, and if they did, what might result if she ever tripped over one. Maybe it would flip into the air, arc above her head and accidentally zap a color onto her. Sister Mim believed that if such a thing ever did happen to happen, she would be perfectly content to have just one color added to her chalkiness and merely a band of it at that, perhaps on her sleeves, because she didn't want to be greedy. And nothing loud, just a humble muddy brown would suffice. That would keep her from becoming unduly proud.

So Sister Mim bargained with her higher power. If just a single zap could be managed on her behalf, she probably wouldn't ever have to ask for anything else again, and she would commit the rest of her life to the advancement of goodness, which she had already been doing for some time by the way, in case it hadn't been noticed. In the meantime, Sister Mim remained rather cross and bossy, emanating cold like a single pane window.

Sister Mim challenged Marmalada Mouse. "What you're proposing isn't suitable," she protested. "And it's not anything we are used to anymore." Then pushing aside her last bit of food, she excused herself so that she could tend to her duties.

Marmalada Mouse dismissed Sister Mim's pooh-poohing with a roll of her eyes and a wave of her hand. "That cupboard," she continued coyly, "isn't someone going to dibs it?" She tried to sound glib and disinterested. It was Dibs Day, the third Thursday of the month. But it wasn't her turn so she could only attempt a claim if the dibbser of the day failed to speak up when the music box ran down, and then she would have to be the first one to call out the word.

Marmalada Mouse's heartbeat accelerated as the music box slowed. And when, at last, it reluctantly gave out its last lethargic plink, she shouted possessively, "DIBS! That cupboard is going to be my house!" Pointing to the shelves with a vigorous thrust of her arm caused her tiara to flop low on her forehead, which it had a tendency to do. "I can see the living room on the lower level, and then a kitchen on the first shelf, and, yes, the bedroom should be …"

She enthusiastically rambled on, and the group followed her finger with their eyes, but no one saw what she saw and none of them wanted to say so, in the same way that nobody wanted to tell her that her floppy tiara often looked more like a miner's head lamp than a queenly adornment. So, acting as if they had important things to do, they excused themselves, and left Marmalada Mouse alone. But not for long.

Owly Professor Fowler overheard Marmalada Mouse.

And he understood her frustration when people didn't catch her vision, because he did. The old Professor spent most of his time dozing on a high beam, but there wasn't anything that could rouse an elderly bird off his perch and make him feel young again like a good idea can, so he was anxious to talk to Marmalada Mouse. He hoped she wouldn't think he was too old to know anything.

"Watch out below!" Professor Fowler sounded the alarm within seconds of his take-off, ruing his decision to attempt an old stunt in an effort to impress Marmalada Mouse. In his younger days he had been famous for his dangerous daredevil-single-wing-spiral-torpedo-dive. Holding one wing to his side while flapping the other in triple time and rapidly jerking his head side-to-side, a technique he called the flippy-whippy, he was able to lift off from the rafters, go into a quasi-freefall and land solidly on his feet.

However, in his present enthusiasm there were a few things he hadn't carefully considered this time, namely, his advanced age, an increase in his poundage, and something tucked under his wing for Marmalada Mouse that threw his balance off.

Missing his mark, he crash landed, went into a somersault, a roll and then a skid that ran him right into Marmalada Mouse. Although she bristled at his rudeness, her irritation quickly gave way to sympathy when she saw Professor Fowler struggling to get to his feet, pretending he wasn't hurt. But when he shimmied his feathers back into place, his grimace gave him away.

Marmalada Mouse recalled his reputation. People said he was wise because of the grand overview he had from living so high near the peak of the roof, and also because he had lived in the attic for such a long time that he had accumulated an extensive collection of informative files. So, while he was still trying to get himself together, she pretended too, pretended to notice a spot on her dress. She slapped at it briskly, looking away from the Professor's discomfort and his ruffled gray plumage that didn't sleek tidily into place anymore. With her eyes averted, she said she was glad he had dropped by because she needed his advice.

"Well, I'll be," the professor said, speaking as if his visit had been happenstance. "Funny you should ask. Believe it or not, under this wing, here, I'm carrying one of my Seven Question Project Planners. And you know, filling out a 7Q Double P is as fun as playing a game. And it only has two rules: Answer all the questions and tell yourself the truth." He handed her the rolled up planner, which had suffered injury as well as he, but he didn't apologize for its rumpled condition.

In light of his newly acquired aches and pains, Professor Fowler resolved to forego any future attempts at cleverness. Nevertheless, he figured Marmalada Mouse had been worth the bruises he had sustained. So he flew back to his perch with a sense of satisfaction, "ow-ow-owing" with every flap of his wings.

Marmalada Mouse smoothed out the creased planner and read out loud.

(1) What do you want to do? (Answer this question in seven words or less.)

(2) What tasks are required to reach your goal? Estimate the time they will take and write them down in order of importance.

(3) Whom would you have to hire and what would you need to buy?

Three practical questions, that's all it took to disinterest Marmalada Mouse. "Ho-hum," she yawned, "this isn't what I call a game, but I better read questions four through seven so I won't be lying when I say I read it from beginning to end. After all, Professor Fowler is very nice and I don't want to hurt his feelings so I just won't tell him that for the time being I'm setting his planner aside." She read on in slapdash fashion, running the questions together:

(4) How much money will each thing cost? Add everything up.

(5) Now count your money. Do you have enough?

(6) If the answer to question five is "no," then how much more will it cost if you get a loan?

(7) Give all of your answers a good review. Now, do you still want to do what you want to do?

"Yes, I do want to do what I want to do." Marmalada Mouse snorted. She crumpled the planner and tossed it aside. Then, feeling a need for distraction, she dropped her pennies into her jewelry bag tote and set off shopping. It was her day to clean for Ella Bouffante, however, so she had to ask for the afternoon off. Ella Bouffante agreed because she actually felt quite at ease amidst the messy amassment of things she had accrued. She was addicted to dibbsing, and sometimes it was hard to distinguish her from her stuff because there was so much of it.

She was quite fat so she largely sat in her brass and copper rocker. And it was Marmalada Mouse's job to keep a clear path to her chair because Ella Bouffante's lap was the first  place youngsters were sent when they arrived at the attic in a state of disrepair. She would wrap her jelloey arms around them as far as they could go and fan their fevered brows with her jumbonic ears and rub their backs with her great trunk. "Mmm, Hmm," she would say, "I know, I know." They leaned into her softness and cried as long as they wanted. And when she sent them on their way she gave them sweets and goodies because she believed that treats alleviated the pain of insults and injuries.

Marmalada Mouse ambled about without any particular plan.

When she decided to turn in at Kids' Toys Road she immediately encountered Bobby Capella dangling in a carton, hanging by his ankles, so that the only visible parts of him were his big yellow shoes. But the sound of his doo-bee-doo-bee-doos, smooth as silk, seemed to ooze right through the cardboard. Bobby Capella sang most of the time and sometimes, when he spotted someone from the corner of his eye, he'd act as if he didn't know they were near, and he'd casually loosen his bow tie and croon louder than usual, adding "yeah" to the end of some lines. He hoped people would tell him that he was good. They often did.

Bobby Capella disappeared into the carton with a kerplunk and Marmalada Mouse waited for him to come back up. But instead, something curious emerged at the top of the box - a tiny living room chair, upholstered in red with black polka dots. It seemed to levitate all by itself.

Then, with a grunt, Bobby Capella popped up like toast from a toaster, the chair teetering on his head, held by a rubber band that went up over its arms and down under his chin. Panting, he asked, "Phew, how d'ya like my hat, ha, ha? Got a matching couch," he wheezed, trying to catch his breath, "and a chest of drawers, hand-built. All sorts of customized stuff. No cheap commercial junk. And to tell you the truth," Bobby Capella said with a wink and a 'tch-tch' from the side of his mouth, "I think some of these goods are downright rare."

"But I'm gonna cut my prices if you're a buyer because I'll be obliged to give you the first-customer-of-the-day deduction. That keeps a bunch of money in your wallet, and if you happen to buy all of it, I'll stand by my discount practice on volume deals and slash my profits." Marmalada Mouse appreciated his generosity.

"Look at this darlin' item," he said, directing her attention with his eyes to the chair balanced on his head. "How many hours do you suppose it took Mr. and Mrs. B to do all that designin' and sawin' and paintin'' and sewin.' Think of the love! Tch-tch. You can't put a price on that, no siree!"

"O-o-oh, I agree," Marmalada Mouse said, nodding vigorously. "Think of the love!"

"Ouch. This little find is getting' heavy," Bobby Capella grimaced. "And I've only got a couple of minutes to get it down and bring all my one-of-a-kind treasures out before people start crowdin' around and puttin' on the pressure and this thing turns into some kind of auction, and then the prices go skyrockettin' on us."

Bobby Capella managed to get the chair down to the floor without mishap. He walked around it, analyzing its lines. "Yes, mighty fine, tch-tch," he assured himself. He pulled a folded handkerchief from his back pocket and with a flick of his wrist, snapped it in the air and began gently dusting the little chair. Marmalada Mouse was mesmerized. He paused and held his other hand to his ear. "Are those footsteps I hear?" he asked.

Marmalada Mouse didn't hear anyone coming, but just in case they were she decided to act fast. "Bobby Capella, I better buy the contents of that box," she said. "You weren't at lunch today when I dibbsed that big cupboard, but I'm going to turn it into a house. So I need a chair and a couch, and probably everything you've got there. But I don't know if I have enough money or if I can move everything by myself."

"Tell you what I'm gonna do, and I'm not accustomed to doin' it." Bobby Capella whispered as if he were telling her a secret. "But for a good customer like you, I'll load it all up in my truck and deliver it for free! Tch-tch. Is that a deal?"

It was a deal! Marmalada Mouse poured out her pennies and Bobby Capella counted. "Say, this looks about right," he assured her. "Maybe you're a little bit shy, but, hey, let's not waste time. I've got to start loadin' now so I can be done before tomorrow mornin.'" He rolled up his sleeves and then patted his back pockets and his empty shirt pocket. "I'll have to give you an itemized receipt later," he said. "I don't seem to have a pencil and paper on me."

Bobby Capella dug his thumbtack cleats into the cardboard carton and punched his way back up to the top of the box. He dropped out of sight before Marmalada Mouse was able to say thanks or goodbye. And there was no use trying. He wouldn't have heard her. He was already crooning loudly about the bloo-oo-oos in the night, yeah.

Marmalada Mouse went back to her nest, skipping most of the way, her heart and her tote as light as air.

At early light, before anyone else roused, Marmalada Mouse hurried to her cupboard.

She was anxious to arrange her fabulous new furniture and stun everyone with a triumphant "ta-dah," without conveying smugness, mind you, just good-old-fashioned positivity. But it was she who was in for a surprise. Up on the first shelf was a big hot-red button tipped on its side, leaning against a wooden "hecho en Mexico" box that was missing its lid. Three more buttons, but all of different color, blue, green and black, lay beside the box, too.

"What possible use could there be for those?" she asked herself with some befuddlement, and she decided not to climb up to investigate further.

But she dug with abandon into the jumble that was at floor level. Fumbling past hankies and miscellaneous cloth remnants that further confounded her, she finally got down to the red upholstered chair. And for the moment, her enthusiasm returned.

But by the time she had uncovered the matching couch and the chest of drawers, she had also discovered a broken earring, a belt buckle, a clear plastic funnel, a yellow pencil and various items she set aside unidentified.

And at the bottom of it all, too heavy for Marmalada Mouse to budge, stood a rusted corpse of a stove without any burners

and no oven door. She didn't look any further. Now the little chair that had seemed so spectacular the day before looked faded and sadly worn.

"Don't let anybody know" was her first self-protective thought. She hastily recrammed the bottom shelf, holding back two hankies to use as draping material to hide everything else and create the look of a future grand opening in progress. That would give her time to deal with Bobby Capella and accumulate some proper furnishings. But how, she wondered. She held her tote upside down and shook it, hoping a few stuck pennies might fall out. But none did. She was broke!

Marmalada Mouse gave in to tears of anger and buyer's remorse. She ran to Ella Bouffante for consolation. "I don't feel good," she lied, falling against Ella Bouffante's pillowiness. But only one of her legs could fit on the little bit of knee that wasn't overlapped by Ella Bouffante's tummy fat. So she grabbed onto Ella Bouffante's great ears to keep from falling and hung there, her free leg flailing in the air and her rump slumping toward the floor. She grunted and tugged and readjusted and tried to make herself small - small enough to fit - small enough for pity.

But Ella Bouffante was unable to accommodate such a sprawl and Marmalada Mouse fell to the floor. "My lap," Ella Bouffante apologized, "I think it's just for the little ones, dear."

Marmalada Mouse still wasn't up to telling the truth so with an insincere "sorry," she scrambled to her feet and trudged back to her nest where she dropped to the floor and boo-hoo-hooed all over her bedding. She wanted to cry for the rest of her life, and she tried to, but she just couldn't make her tears last. So she got up and spread out her shreds to dry so that she wouldn't have to sleep in a damp bed that night.

However, Marmalada Mouse was too upset to be her usual reasonable self. She threw them and kicked at them. "Stupid shreds!" she said. Then, snatching up a crumpled sheet of paper, she methodically tore it into bits and flung the whole lot of them into the air. With tight lips and arms folded hard against her chest, she sat down and watched them flutter like falling autumn leaves. But one stray scrap caught a draft, and it wafted up and spun around and then went into a slow spiral. Marmalada Mouse followed its path with her eyes and her head, circling, circling, circling, until it settled lightly on her lap. Now that scrap happened to have three words on it. And it landed right side up.

Marmalada Mouse focused in on the print and read those three words: *get a loan*. "Oh, no!" she whispered to herself, recalling the phrase. "I've destroyed Professor Fowler's Planner!" The Planner. She hadn't meant to ruin it, but there it was strewn in little bits all over the room. And yet - this seemed a brilliant thought - one single snippet out of, oh, say, at least the million that she must have tossed, this very particular snippet was the one and only one to practically fall right out of the sky and land smack dab in the middle of her lap! It had to be a lucky sign. Get a loan! That was the answer to her problems. She went to see Tom Purrdy.

"Meow do you do Marmalada Mouse?"

Tom Purrdy tipped his hat and invited her to sit down to chat at his worktable. "Purrmit me to clean a penny while we talk," he said. Without waiting for her permission, he lifted a coin from a stack of dull pennies and seemed to get lost in his polishing.

Marmalada Mouse watched him. Tom was a rather tacky knickknack. His right leg was too long, so a blob of hard glue had been daubed onto the bottom of his left foot to keep him from falling over when he stood up. His purple coat had grayed and his long stringy whiskers dangled limply. He had doffed his hat so often that his pudgy paw prints were permanently smudged into its brim. Marmalada Mouse didn't think he looked like a rich person ought to, but the truth of it was, he had more pennies than anybody else in the attic.

And that wasn't by accident. Tom Purrdy kept track of every penny that came into his possession. Each was assigned a purpose and then put into its particular purpose pile where it stayed until there was a right time to spend it. And those piles never got mixed up because Tom Purrdy had labeled them as carefully as Mrs. B had her attic boxes.

Marmalada Mouse noted with distaste that his shortest money pile was labeled "New Hat," and she decided that he needed a slight nudge toward better grooming. "You know," she said with a knowledgeable air and an instructive point of an index finger, "If you take some pennies from that 'Sharing' pile there and some from your 'Saving' pile and transfer them to your 'New Hat' pile, I would be happy to shop for you."

"Sharing and saving are priorities to me, Marmalada Mouse," he said, unmoved by her suggestion. "So I don't fuss with those piles. And a new hat isn't in their league, at least not yet. He held up a gleaming coin and admired his work. "Take a look. Now, that's what I call purrdy! Ha, ha. Get the joke?"

"Yes, I get the joke," Marmalada Mouse said. "And that's what I want to do, too - make things purrdy!" Then she told him in one long sentence about dibbsing the cupboard and about the furnishings she bought and about the junk she inadvertently got on account of Bobby Capella not being all that honest but she didn't want to talk about that right now, she just wanted to get a start on her project and, by the way, did he have two hundred and fifty pennies she could borrow.

Tom Purrdy took a lazy stretch, extending his arms high, and then resting his paws on the top of his head. "Now, Marmalada Mouse," he began thoughtfully, "I know how Bobby Capella operates. You say he was kind enough to deliver for free. Well, that's unusual because ordinarily he charges a rental fee for the use of his vehicle. And, Marmalada Mouse, that's what borrowing money is all about. You rent it pretty much like you rent a truck." Tom pulled a stack of coins close to himself. "Now, these are all mine," he said, hugging the pile. "But, if I let you take them for your new house, I can't count them or polish them or spend them myself. So, I'd ask you to pay a fee for all the fun I miss out on while they're gone. Does that make sense to you?"

"Interesting explanation," Marmalada Mouse said.

"Yes, it is interest …"

"How much of a fee?" Marmalada Mouse blurted, before he could finish his sentence.

"Okay," Tom Purrdy responded. "Now, let's keep this very simple. Say I lend you 240 pennies for a rental fee of five purrcent, which is 12 pennies. I think that's fair. That comes to a total of 252. So, every month for twelve months you pay me back just 21 of those pennies and in the year's time you will have paid me back both the original 240 and the five purrcent."

Marmalada Mouse was about to speak, but Tom Purrdy put up a paw to stop her. "Now, I must mention that there is one thing more. And I want to be purrfectly clear here. You must give security on a loan. That means you'd have to agree before I could lend you any money that if for some reason, good or bad, you couldn't or didn't pay the pennies back, I'd get something you own instead. Something good. And it would be understood between you and me from the get-go just what that something would be. And I'll say right now, I could make good use of those shelves."

"A-a-a-and," he continued, hushing Marmalada Mouse one more time, "Monthly payments are expected on a definite day, mmm, let's say the tenth of the month. And if you didn't pay by then, I'd have to charge you a late fee, and after five days, if you still haven't paid, I'd get to either call the remaining amount of the loan due or take the shelves, whichever I choose."

Tom Purrdy expected Marmalada Mouse to change her mind after getting all of that information. He put his elbows on the table and held his paws close to his nose, rhythmically tapping his claws as he waited for her response. She put an elbow on the table, too, and rested her chin in her hand. "Well, I wouldn't want to lose those shelves." She thought out loud. "Let's see. When I rent a truck, I pay a fee. I use the truck and then I give it back. And that's the end of that." She slowed down a bit. "But, if I borrow money, I borrow it so I can spend it. So I spend it. And then it's gone. How do I return something that's gone?" She paused. Tom Purrdy continued to tap his claws. "Well," she finally said. "I guess I would just work more and pay you from the extra money I earn." Satisfied with herself, Marmalada Mouse folded her hands and rested them on her lap, anticipating good news.

"Now, you're on the right track, Marmalada Mouse, and that's terrific," Tom Purrdy assured her. "But, we need to get much more specific here. What work will you do, and for whom? And how many hours at what pay? It wouldn't be wise for me to lend, or for you to borrow without answers to those questions. Purrhaps you might confer with Professor Fowler and come back with a financial plan."

That wasn't what Marmalada Mouse wanted to hear, especially since she had already decided that the boredom of planning destroyed her spontaneity and squelched her artistic spirit. She resented the practicalities that seemed to stifle her dream. "Well, I'll get back to you then," she said, forcing her mouth into a wide line that she hoped would pass for a smile. She turned, disgruntled, toward her corner. It was late that night when Marmalada Mouse finally gathered up the shreds she had angrily thrown around. She fluffed them into a pile, nosed in, and lay down for the night.

"Psst. Psst." Marmalada Mouse woke to someone trying to get her attention.

She poked her nose out of her shreds and heard the "psst" again. Then she sat up at the whisper of her name. When Tom Purrdy appeared, seemingly out of nowhere, she jumped to her feet.

"Shh! don't be afraid," he whispered, "I think I was too hard on you today and I've come tonight with a change of mind. Look in here," he said, beckoning with a curl of his claw. Marmalada Mouse stepped hesitantly toward him and peered into the tattered bag he had brought with him, hoping it held pennies. When she saw that it was filled with beebees, she took a wary step back.

"Now, here's how this borrowing game works," he said. "Debt is something a person carries. So, you borrow a penny, you carry a beebee. Borrow two pennies, you carry two beebees. Borrow three, four, five … you get where I'm going?"

"Yes," Marmalada Mouse said. "I get it, but may I transfer those beebees to my fashionable jewelry bag tote?"

"And how will you carry it?" he asked.

Marmalada Mouse put an arm through one of the drawstring loops, flipped the bag onto her back and slipped her other arm through the second loop. "See. It fits just like Lissa's and Jimmy's backpacks," she said.

"A jewelry bag backpack. It's purrfect. I wish I had thought of it myself," Tom Purrdy said. "Now, when you make purrchases," he continued, "just tell the sellers to come to me to get paid because you've left all of your pennies with me for polishing. Then you get to work, and every month when you make a payment of 21 pennies, I'll relieve you of 21 beebees.

And if you count them every week and compare your numbers with mine, we'll always know how much you owe."

"Now, I'm breaking my own rules for you, here, Marmalada Mouse," he said, "so let's keep these details a secret between just you and me." She nodded in agreement.

Then he gave her a pen and pointed to a line on a paper and asked for her signature. There was so little light that it was hard for Marmalada Mouse to see exactly where to put her name, so she signed at the very bottom of the page.

Tom Purrdy tucked the paper in his hat and blended back into the darkness as mysteriously as he had appeared. And Marmalada Mouse took off her pack, loaded it with beebees and slung it back on.

The sound of Mrs. B opening the hatch sent everyone into hiding.

A scheduled meeting at the Big Broad Way had to be delayed because she came and went so many times, depositing two or more cartons on every trip, and leaving a total of ten new boxes on Kid's Toys Road alone. "I wish I were an octopus," Marmalada Mouse thought. "I could grab eight handfuls at a time and no one would stop me."

But since Marmalada Mouse was merely a mouse, she had to rely on her charm and wits. So when the meeting finally started and the leader asked if there was any new business, she made a ridiculous suggestion in the guise of a proposal meant for everyone's benefit. "Because of this new surplus of goods in the attic, I think it would behoove all of us to have Dibs Day more often. Therefore, I move that we dibs every single day." Her tactic of over-proposing worked. Somebody countered that weekly dibbsing might be more reasonable and after a lively debate, they finally came to that agreement.

So, Marmalada Mouse's routine changed that day. She quit working for Ella Bouffante in order to put all of her efforts toward her cupboard project. She diligently dibbsed and followed closely behind others as they did, buying up every treasure she could. Deciding that Bobby Capella's sofa and chair were now way too plain, she replaced them with flowery overstuffed couches. And she abandoned her feathers and shreds for a regal four-poster bed. Carpeting ran from wall to wall on every floor and draperies and chandeliers hung in every room. Her china cabinet was aburst with silver service and porcelain cups that she brought out for tours and teas when she wanted to show off her stockpile of finery.

And eventually, Marmalada Mouse became so enamored with stuff that she couldn't find a stopping point. There was always one more thing needed to complete a collection, to create ambience, to provide greater efficiency or to merely please the eye. And keeping up with her new appetite required more borrowing which she didn't want to think about, so she neglected the discipline of her weekly beebee count and payment schedule, which in turn added to the debt she owed and, consequently, the number of beebees she was required to carry in her backpack.

However, Marmalada Mouse did not discern the true impact of her actions because a person gets used to extra weight when it comes in tiny increments of one or two beebees at a time. Besides, she had good intentions. She went to bed every night with resolve to get her finances in order the very next day. But, somehow, and always with seemingly good reasons, "the very next day" came and went many times with no resolution.

Then one day, Tom Purrdy dropped by unexpectedly. "Now, Marmalada Mouse," he said without the usual courtesy of removing his hat. "I'm not here for just one monthly payment as you probably expect. Many of your payments have been late, as you well know, and this time you are six days past the five-day grace period, so I've come to get the balance due of 410 pennies."

But Marmalada Mouse had handled beebees for such a long time she didn't think in terms of pennies anymore. "You mean 410 beebees," she said correctively.

"No, Marmalada Mouse," he said. "You don't owe me beebees. You owe me pennies."

Marmalada Mouse swallowed hard as if beebees were stuck in her throat. "Please, sit down," she croaked, gesturing toward her most comfortable chair.

"No thanks-s-s, he said flatly.

Marmalada Mouse didn't think Tom Purrdy sounded like himself. "Please, sit, sit, sit," she insisted in a slightly flirty way, patting the cushion of the chair. Smiling and blinking rapidly, she hoped to charm the unfamiliar hiss out of Tom Purrdy's voice. "I'll be back in just one teensy minute," she said. And then she ran to her bedroom where a few pennies were hidden under her four-poster bed. She counted. She counted again. But she couldn't come up with more than seven. She bagged them in a hairnet anyway, gathered her composure and her skirt, and sashayed back to the living room, dragging the pennies behind her.

She smiled at Tom Purrdy and sank limply onto a settee. But since her backpack took up so much of the seat, she ended up in a lean rather than a sit. Pretending that she always draped herself against furniture that way, she proceeded to fan her face and say with a sigh, "This has been such a strenuous ordeal for me, but my project is almost complete as I am sure you can see." She raised her arm and made a slow wide arc in a gesture of grand presentation. And then as a deflective ploy she offered him some tea. "And do take these seven coins," she added dismissively, as if they were an annoyance. "In no time at all, I'll be bringing you the remaining, uh, would that be 293?"

"No, three hundred and ninety three." he said. "Now, Marmalada Mouse," he continued, "Since you haven't kept your word, lending to you has become very ris-s-sky. So, here is the only thing I am willing to do for you. I will take these pennies off your hands and rent you the remaining 393 at sixty purrcent.

"Sixty percent! I can't pay that kind of rent," Marmalada Mouse cried.

"You mus-s-s-t, you must pay that rent. And if you don't," he threatened, "I'll pounce on your hous-s-s-e!" Tom Purrdy removed his hat and Marmalada Mouse saw that the blacks of his eyes had turned to dollar signs.

"And there is another matter, Marmalada Mouse," Tom Purrdy said. "I've covered purrchases made beyond your borrowing limit, so you'll have to add more beebees to your pack. Marmalada Mouse noticed the bulging bag that lay at his feet, and she attempted to challenge him, but he pulled a list from the crown of his hat, along with receipts, for a lamp, a flower arrangement, miscellaneous items and more miscellaneous items.

"I … I … I had no idea … no idea that things could add up that … that fast," she whimpered.

Tom Purrdy put his hat back on. "They add up fas-s-st when you don't keep track, when you get so scared that you turn your back on the facts-s-s." He rubbed his paws together gleefully. "And as per the teensy-weensy print at the bottom of our contract, I have to remind you that in addition to the late fee, you have also incurred a presumptuous purrchase surcharge, a foolhardy fine, a secrecy fee, a greedy pig penalty and a reassessment assessment."

"Small print?" Marmalada Mouse asked. She looked up at him with pleading eyes. "It was dark, and I didn't really read the contract, and I thought you were being so nice!"

She hoped he would decide to be kind, but Tom Purrdy just smirked and shook his head in disrespect at her carelessness. Then he counted out the beebees Marmalada Mouse would have to carry on her back, and left without saying goodbye.

Her pack strained at the seams, unable to accommodate its new burden.

But, since all those beebees had to be carried one way or another, Marmalada Mouse slipped some into the hem of her dress and filled her pocket and the toes of her shoes. Consequently, she lost her freedom that day. It hurt to walk. She tripped over her dress that now stretched to the floor. She ached from the weight of the pack on her back. It all became too much to bear with any sense of self-possession, and she became edgy and irritable and lost her creative drive. So Marmalada Mouse took to her bed where she lay for hours at a time sighing wearily.

One evening as she languished there, staring out the dormer window, she noticed two seemingly unrelated things, a heavy black sky promising a storm and a fray in the seam of her bulging backpack. They came together in an odd idea, an idea that a dishonest person would hop right onto, but one that an honest person would readily dismiss, but also an idea that can catch a good person by surprise when she is in trouble. And when that person feels trapped, panic may rob her of her usual good sense so that she doesn't get advice or think the problem through carefully on her own. Instead, she acts rashly and stupidly, as Marmalada Mouse was about to do.

She picked at the fray, tugging lightly on a stretched thread as if to test it. But she kept at it until it finally broke. (It was then that she knew for sure she was going to do what she was going to do.) Carefully hoisting her pack to her back, she slowly plodded toward the downstairs-access corner. She glanced furtively in every direction to be sure no one was paying undue attention to her, and pretended busyness when someone seemed to be looking her way. When she finally got to the corner, she lowered her backpack into the in-between space between the downstairs ceiling and the attic floor where she began to transfer beebees from her pocket into her already-tautly-stretched tote. "It was his idea," she grumbled, jamming beebees into the bag, "to put these things," she jammed some more, "in my pack!" Another thread snapped.

And when a jagged white stab of light flashed across the black sky, she forced the beebees harder and faster, knowing that thunder would momentarily follow. Her timing was good. Just as a reverberating boom rattled the windows, her backpack burst, and thunder swallowed the ping of tiny metal spheres bouncing into the irretrievable darkness inside the wall.

Her bag exploded before she could empty her hem and the toes of her shoes, however, so there was no spring in Marmalada Mouse's step when she hobbled her way back to see Tom Purrdy. Plus her head throbbed with self justification as she rehearsed her rationalization over and over, convincing herself that her brand new and very literal interpretation of Tom Purrdy's backpack instructions was valid. "Put them in the backpack." That's what he had said. And that's what she had done.

Hoping to elicit sympathy, Marmalada Mouse exaggerated her stagger as she approached Tom Purrdy. Laying her torn and empty bag on his polishing table, she hunched her shoulders up, held her empty hands out and cocked her head in a pretense of helplessness. "There's no way I can account for those beebees now," she said, hoping she had one-upped Tom Purrdy. And then she employed a downstairs word she thought would be her clincher, a word she didn't think he thought she knew. "Correct me if I'm wrong," she said, trying to hide her nervousness, "but I don't believe people are required to pay back their loans after they've experienced the trauma of bagrupturancy."

Tom Purrdy was so unimpressed that he didn't bother to correct her pronunciation or her perception. Suddenly his dollar-sign eyes began to spin like pinwheels and his whiskers sprang to life, undulating like octopus tentacles, groping at Marmalada Mouse. "I see you've chosen the easy way out," he said. "But, what you do not know, Marmalada Mouse, is that in this life there is no - I repeat - there is no such thing as an easy way out. You're going to have to plead your so-called 'bagrupturancy' case in court!"

Pastor Myron, the pottery preacher, prepared to act as judge.

He and his clerical clothes were sculpted from a single hunk of clay, so his robe was as much a part of him as his skin; he was what he wore and he wore what he was. Pastor Myron was kind, as pastors should be, but he was unaware of his condescending air, as well as his habit of dominating most conversations with serious monologues. Plus, he had a comb-over and his favorite composer was Bach, so it's understandable that Pastor Myron wasn't very popular. He sensed the tendency of people to back away from him and camouflaged his loneliness by always holding a big open book against his belly and acting as if he were engrossed in its subject matter.

However, his ministerial attire and demeanor seemed to qualify him for the unusual civic occasion at hand and he was glad to offer his services. Stepping up onto a box, he proudly took the oath of office and promised to uphold the law, so help him God.

"Order in the court-ourt-ourt," he demanded. His voice caromed off the attic walls in a double echo. "Marmalada Mouse-ouse-ouse. Approach the bench-ench-ench," he commanded. "I have a question to ask you-ask-you-ask-you." Marmalada Mouse obeyed. She slowly tipped her head back and looked up into his face.

"Marmalada Mouse-ouse-ouse," he repeated. "If one person has something that belongs to someone else-else-else, and that first person doesn't return it as agreed, but keeps it-eeps-it-eeps-it." He bent down until his face almost touched hers and the power of his voice blew her whiskers back until they touched her ears. "How does that differ from stealing-ealing-ealing?"

This wasn't the bland Pastor Myron Marmalada Mouse knew. He pelted her with rapid-fire questions that stung like snowballs in the face and she didn't have time to be clever. Scarcely finding her voice, she confessed that yes, she could have mended her pack and yes, she meant to pay the money back, she really truly intended to pay.

"Your intentions," Pastor Myron said, cutting her off abruptly, "are invisible to this court-ourt-ourt. They can only be judged by someone much more powerful than I-I-I." He paused piously and lifted his eyes in the direction of the sky. "What this court is qualified to judge is your behavior-avior-avior."

Then suddenly his face grew huge and cruel as he pressed his nose against hers. Marmalada Mouse's eyes crossed. "You," he bellowed, "have spent somebody else's money-oney-oney, without a budget or a plan-an-an, and you can't get away with that in this attic-attic-attic!"

Pastor Myron stretched taller and taller as he stood back up. The sun cast his shadow long and dark over Marmalada Mouse. His voice temporarily lost its echo and seemed to come from far, far away. "The sentence of the court is this: You must pay back every last penny. Until you do, Tom Purrdy gets the shelves. Within the hour you must empty them onto the floor. You may keep your bed and your quilt, but you are required to lend everything else you own to any and all of us who ask. You may not demand that we bring anything back." Down came his face one last time, his voice reverberating like a huge brass gong. "You are sentenced to depend-end-end on our good intentions-entions-entions!" Then Pastor Myron did something he had never done. He slammed his book shut. "This court is now adjourned-urned-urned-urned," he pronounced.

Everyone turned against Marmalada Mouse that day. They gathered around as she emptied her house. "Marmalada Mouse doesn't return what she borrows," someone said. "Let's see how she likes it when we do that to her."

"Yeah, yeah," they meanly agreed. "Marmalada Mouse, we want to borrow your chairs. And we want to borrow your dishes. And we want to borrow your couches and your vases and your chandeliers."

Marmalada Mouse wrapped herself up in her quilt, the only comfort she had left in the world, and ventured to ask, "Will anyone ever bring anything back?"

"Oh, we intend to," they taunted in unison. Marmalada Mouse pulled the covers over her head to muffle the derision that had turned into a chant. "We intend to. We intend to!"

The taunting droned on until Marmalada Mouse couldn't take it any longer. She threw off the quilt. "Please," she whimpered. But she was talking to the air because no one was there. Confused, she blinked hard and looked again. Still, no one was there. And, beside that, it was dark! But, how could that be? Her trial had taken place in the morning! Marmalada Mouse grabbed for her quilt only to find feathers and shreds in her hands. And, she wasn't sitting on a four-poster bed either. She was panting and sweating in her old familiar nest. Marmalada Mouse had awakened from a nightmare.

But was it only the trial that had disturbed her sleep? Or did she still owe Tom Purrdy more money than she could ever pay back? Marmalada Mouse wiggled her toes and felt roominess in her shoes. She jumped to her feet and found that her dress didn't drag on the floor. Then she grabbed her tote and turned it over and over looking for the tear. It wasn't there. "That means I never got the loan," she whispered to herself. "And that means I never bought all that stuff. And that means I didn't go through bagrup …" She couldn't make herself finish the word.

It had all been a nightmare, she concluded - the cupboard, Bobby Capella's stuff, spending herself into debt, Pastor Myron's odd behavior, her friends turning on her, everything - just an awful nightmare. Her tight shoulders dropped with relief, and she swore off grand aspirations. Forget about decorations and bouquets and furniture arrangements. Almost having a dream was all the excitement she would ever need.

Marmalada Mouse turned toward the dormer windows and strained to find light in the night sky. It was raining, but moon glow slipped between clouds as they passed by and intermittently lit the windowpanes. She had learned to depend on that window to tell her where she was and to assure her that she was safe when she awakened, afraid in the night. But this time there was no comfort. Wide-eyed, she grimly traced the perimeter of a tall corner cupboard, outlined in pale eerie light.

Marmalada Mouse ran frantically across the attic on heavy feet, forgetting to tiptoe. (Her friends had long since learned to sleep through noises in the night, however, because no one had ever wanted to tell her that she wasn't as light on her feet as she supposed.) She skidded to a stop and was confronted by hankie drapes, the ones she, herself, had hung to hide her stuff and keep her secret. The cupboard was not empty.

So, whatever else may have disappeared upon her waking, one fact remained - she was still stuck with Bobby Capella's junk. Marmalada Mouse dragged back to her nest. Too weary to burrow and unable to sleep, she sat with bowed head and slumped shoulders waiting for sunrise, when she would face up to Professor Fowler.

Marmalada Mouse cupped her hands around her mouth, tipped her head toward the rafters, and chirped a "yoo-hoo."

"Who-hoo-hoo's calling?" Professor Fowler asked. "I'm just getting ready to take my morning nap."

"Marmalada Mouse," she said, struggling to keep her courage so that she could tell the truth. "Er, um, you know that cupboard project of mine? Well, I've made some blunders, and I'll understand if you get mad, but I have to confess I disregarded your planner and, well, now I'm in a serious jam."

"Marmalada Mouse?" he yawned. "I need coffee."

Marmalada Mouse immediately perked up and was about to pour from her miniature saltshaker coffee pot when it struck her that she should put out a little extra effort and do something special for the Professor. She called to him again. "I think I'll go downstairs. It won't take too long. I can tell by the aroma this morning that Mrs. B is brewing a dark roast and she usually has sourdough toast and leaves the crust. I can get that for us, too. Do you want cream? And I'll tip over the sugar bowl if you like sweet."

It had been a long time since Professor Fowler had enjoyed downstairs food. "Black, he answered, "just black. But, speaking of being in a jam, get me some if you can."

Marmalada Mouse grabbed up an eyedropper and her jewelry bag and made her way downstairs. With a good shove on the cabinet door, she was out from under the sink and onto the kitchen floor. She raced to the nook where Mrs. B usually drank her coffee in her ladder-back chair next to an old country spool table. She escaladed the table leg and pulled herself up onto the table top where she found just what she wanted, Mrs. B's cup with coffee still in it.

Marmalada Mouse filled the eyedropper. Then she mounded up some jammy crusts, wrapped them in a piece of napkin and packed up her jewelry bag, slinging it over one shoulder. However, Marmalada Mouse forgot to be her usual careful self and she lingered for a quick swipe of jam right there on the spot. Consequently, she didn't hear the scuff of slippers against the kitchen floor, and it was too late to run when Mrs. B's shadow fell across the table. Marmalada Mouse dropped her hands to her sides and quit blinking her eyes.

When Mrs. B reached for her cup, she jumped at the surprise before her. Puzzled, she sat down and put on the reading glasses that hung on a cord around her neck. She studied her unexpected guest. "One of the kids must have brought you down from the attic," she said to Marmalada Mouse. "But why didn't I notice you when I first sat down? And, what is this mess?" Mrs. B shrugged her shoulders and with a "humph" proceeded to tidy the kitchen. She stood Marmalada Mouse in the greenhouse window above the sink, donned her bib apron and submerged the morning dishes in hot soapy water. Marmalada Mouse stood as still as a statuette except for her knees that jumped uncontrollably under her dress.

And then the doorbell rang. Mrs. B hastily half dried her hands on the front of her apron, peeled it off over her head and tossed it aside as she hurried toward the living room to answer the door. Her apron landed in the sink. Marmalada Mouse moved into action. Dropping from the windowsill to the countertop, she searched for a way of escape, her trusty shoes providing traction and stability as she traversed the slick counter top. Observing that one of the apron ties was dangling, and almost touching the floor, she gave it a tug, and then a pull, and then a hard yank. It didn't budge. The apron, heavily soaked by then, had become an anchor and Marmalada Mouse knew she could hang from the tie safely.

When she heard Mrs. B say "Why don't you stay for a cup of tea," there was no time to waste. Facing the sink, Marmalada

Mouse straddled the apron tie and clutched it with both hands, one in front of her and one behind. Then she backed to the front edge of the counter, pressed her feet against its edge and bent her knees. "Here I go," she yodeled with a dry throat. Pushing off, Marmalada Mouse repelled the cabinet face and within a few seconds she was on the floor. And in a second more, she was under the sink behind the cabinet door. Then, as fast as she had ever gone, Marmalada Mouse made a run for home.

Marmalada Mouse was out of breath when she pulled herself up onto the attic floor.

She slouched in the corner, panting. In her flight, the eyedropper had dribbled dry and the buttery crusts had fallen from her jewelry bag - she had lost the Professor's snacks. Unwilling to face him right away with a second failure, Marmalada Mouse made unnecessary detours to delay her return.

She happened upon Minny Diminuette on Paper Backs Cul de Sac. Minny Diminuette was a mouse, too, but of a different breed. She was a research mouse, a perky squeak of a creature who wore yellow-framed glasses that magnified her eyes. She had to climb up onto a book to read it and skip across its pages to follow the lines, and she always underlined words she encountered for the first time. Words were her friends, and feeling sorry for the ones that didn't get used very much, she tried to give them their due. Consequently, they often tumbled out of her mouth in contrived combinations.

Marmalada Mouse presumptuously sat on the page Minny Diminuette was reading. "Well, greetings, my dear," Minny Diminuette said in surprise. "What a..." she paused, searching her brain for a neglected word. "What a gladsome inexpectation," she said, "and what is the status of your well being?" Marmalada Mouse said "fine" without meaning it, and immediately recounted all of her troubles.

Minny Diminuette listened patiently with interested my-oh-mys. "Your nettlesome dream episode, my dear, is commonplace," she said. In fact I have written an essay on that very subject entitled 'The Nightmare of Debt: A Double Flabbergastation.' Its astonishment is found in the fact that it occurs both in and outside the somnolent state."

Unfamiliar vocabulary stopped Marmalada Mouse down and the blacks of her eyes turned into tiny exes, so Minny Diminuette decided to limit her use of odd phraseologizations and speak in plainer terms. "The nightmare can occur when you're awake or asleep," she clarified.

Marmalada Mouse's eyes went back to normal, her pupils opening wide with interest, so Minny Diminuette continued. "But this is how they differ," she said. "When you're asleep, you can't prevent having a nightmare. And that's bad. But, the moment you wake up, poof, it's gone. And that's good. Conversely, you do have the power to prevent the real-life nightmare from happening at all. And that's good. However, you can also, by your very own careless actions, create it. And if you do, there is no poof. There is no magic. It will not vanish. And, my, oh my, that is very, very bad."

Minny Diminuette narrowed her eyes like a snake and slinked around Marmalada Mouse. The nightmare was like a leech, she told her, slithering underneath a person's eyelids to keep them from shutting like they should and making them pop open all through the night. And every time they popped, she said, one end of the creepy thing would sink deeper into the person's brain until it sucked onto the replay button so the person could only think of bill collectors, payments due and overdue, extra fees, late charges, bill collectors and payments due ... On and on it would drone, and the person would try to muffle the sound with a pillow and beg for sleep that the sinister wiggler would only give the person in little fitful bits. The same thing went on during the day, she said, so that the person was afraid to open the mail, or answer the phone or open the door.

But that wasn't the end of the misery. The real-life nightmare was like a thug, she said, sitting on the bed, slapping the exhausted person upside the head early in the morning. "Aay," the bad guy would say, "Youse godda gimme credit, buddy-boy. I'm da' best friend youse eva had! Tink a' all dat stuff youse got becuz uh' me. And tink a' all doze clevah lies and excuooses I taught youse to say when people call youse up about doze balances doo. So don't youse go fuhgettin' dat I'm da boss of youse. Now get off da' bed. Moove! It ain't gonna kill youse to woik twoo, tree jobs!"

Then Minny Diminuette resumed her own cheerful voice. "But, believe it or not, defeating that beastful beast is actually a simple matter if a person wants to be strong."

Marmalada Mouse could hardly believe her ears. Her face and heart brightened. "Oh, I do want to be strong," she said, "Especially if it's easy!"

Minny Diminuette gave Marmalada Mouse a quizzical look. "Either I misspoke or you misheard, my dear. I believe I used the word 'simple,' meaning uncomplicated, not 'easy,' meaning an absence of effort." That got Minny Diminuette sidetracked. "You know, my dear," she offered as an aside, "I wrote another essay that speaks directly to that distinction. It is a paper I titled, 'Slack, Sapless, Flabby Abs: Aftermath of Taking the Easy Road.' Ah, but I mustn't digress. That's for another day. Back to the subject at hand."

Minny Diminuette sat down next to Marmalada Mouse and patted her on the knee. "You know, my dear." She spoke kindly, but enunciated carefully. "There are many ways to be strong in life. But none of them is easy."

And then Minny Diminuette offered Marmalada Mouse one more comparison. "To increase muscle power, a person lifts weights," she said. "The heavier the weights get, the stronger the person becomes. But the opposite is true for the person carrying debt. Remember in your dream how those beebees just wore you down, just wore you out? It's decreasing that load - decreasing it - that will give you back your strength."

Minny Diminuette could have gone on about the value of research and mentors, the necessity of discipline and follow through and the benefits of accountability. There was so much she could have said, but too much information at one time, even if it were good and true, would be overwhelming. "Just open the door slightly," she thought to herself. "Let Marmalada Mouse look into the light a little bit at a time."

(She did decide, however, that it would be negligence on her part if she didn't drop Marmalada Mouse a note explaining the Probable Law of 1=3. As a first-time dreamer, Marmalada Mouse would have no idea to expect that when a project is supposed to cost a penny, it will probably cost three. And, likewise, if a job is scheduled to take an hour, it will probably take three.)

Reverting to her histrionic self, Minny Diminuette stood back up. Lifting her pencil high in the air as if it were a torch in the night, she proclaimed, "Oh, the tired, the worn-out person yearning to be free," And then she couldn't resist just one more admonition. "Marmalada Mouse, I think it would behoove …" Minny Diminuette stopped mid-sentence without making her point. "Behoo-oo-oove." She said the word again, letting the o-o-o swirl deliciously in her mouth before letting the word go. "That is a superb word. Do you know? …"

"I know that one!" Marmalada Mouse assured her. "I like that word, too."

Marmalada Mouse left Paperbacks Cul de Sac with a lot on her mind.

She turned backwards to wave goodbye and smacked right into Pastor Myron. He wasn't watching where he was going either, being preoccupied as usual with his big open book. But he was the one to apologize. However, she wanted to stay mad at Pastor Myron for being one of the meanest meanies of all in her nightmare, so she crabbily overreacted to the impact.

Rubbing the back of her head as if she had sustained real injury, Marmalada Mouse admitted to herself that she should probably forgive Pastor Myron for all of the evil things he hadn't actually done. "I'm fine," she said reluctantly. "Oh, it's probably my fault, too. I've been so preoccupied. You see, I made a purchase..." Marmalada Mouse began another recitation of her predicament, but since Pastor Myron wasn't a good listener and could only think clearly when he was the one talking, he took over the conversation.

"You bought a lot of something. It was a mistake. And now you regret it, right? Right!" (Pastor Myron usually answered his own questions.) "And now you wish it would all go away, correct?" Pastor Myron's "uh-huh" overpowered Marmalada Mouse's "mm-hmm."

He began to nod his head slowly and sincerely. "Well, Marmalada Mouse," he continued. "We learn from our mistakes, don't we?" Marmalada Mouse found herself nodding along with him. "Yes we do," he answered for her. "We learn a lot from them."

Pastor Myron's head changed direction. He moved it side to side slowly and sincerely. "We learn because we don't easily forget when things hurt us, do we?" Marmalada Mouse couldn't tell if she was supposed to shake her head in agreement or nod, so she did both. "No, we don't," he answered a third time for her. Pastor Myron's head stopped as he pointed an instructive finger in the air. "But we have to face them, Marmalada Mouse."

Then, once again, he resumed his slow and sincere nodding. She did, too. "We have to lean into them a little bit, find out what they have to teach us." And then Pastor Myron felt moved to tell her something that he himself didn't quite understand at the moment, but he was sure he had received an inspiration. Narrowing his lips and eyes in earnestness, making a soft fist that signified a strong amen, and nodding of course, he counseled her. "Give it some time, Marmalada Mouse. Keep that stuff. Keep it. There's more there than you think. You just haven't looked at it long enough yet." Pastor Myron liked having something important to say. It filled his heart with benevolence. He looked at her affectionately and said, "Call on me any time." And then with a sugary "Buh-by," Pastor Myron continued on his way, his head held high.

Marmalada Mouse's eyes were sloshing like water in a juggler's jar after all that nodding and shaking, so she steadied herself with a straight arm against a carton until she could get her bearings. Then she headed directly to her tardy appointment with Professor Fowler.

"Oh, boy, this doesn't look very good," Professor Fowler muttered.

Marmalada Mouse made her way toward him, dragging her empty jewelry bag. She let the bag drop to the floor and then she did, too. Sitting with her elbows on her knees and her chin in her hands, she told the Professor about her escape from the kitchen window and her encounters with Minny Diminuette and Pastor Myron.

Professor Fowler graciously replaced the 7Q Double P she had tossed aside in spite of the fact that she hadn't delivered his much anticipated treats. "And should you choose to read it," he said with a little sarcasm, "here is one of my Four Question Puzzlers. And the trick in this particular 4QP is that there are several possible answers to each question, but only one answer to each and all of them."

"But, but," Marmalada Mouse protested. "How can there be just one and more than one at the same time?"

"Figure it out," he said sternly. "You have been careless, Marmalada Mouse. But it isn't too late for a new beginning." He spread his wings to fly off, but lingered in a low hover. "I am expecting good things from you," he said reassuringly. Then off he went.

Marmalada Mouse accepted Professor Fowler's rebuke and hung her hopes on his confidence. She flattened her legs into a vee and put the papers on the floor between them, and decided to read the 4QP first because it was quite a bit shorter than the 7Q Double P.

Leaning forward, she read the puzzler:

What do you like to do? What do you do well? Do you do anything that no one else is doing? What would people pay you to do for them?"

Marmalada Mouse forgot for a moment that there was a puzzle to be solved at all because the questions in themselves were so delightful. They were all about her. And she knew all the answers.

"I like to sleep, eat, and be with my friends," she said to herself, considering question one. "I like sitting near the vents so I can smell the seasons. I really like the downstairs, especially when children are there, and I like to bring back downstairs food and good news."

And as she was talking to herself about herself, a sudden whir, a blur, and the sound of laughter swirled around Marmalada 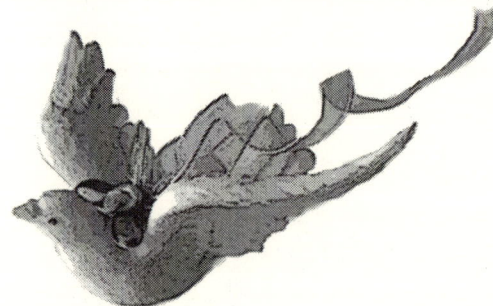 Mouse like a benign tornado. It was Lovey Dovey. Pastel pink and feather fancy with satin roses and velveteen leaves attached to the shoulders of her outstretched wings, Lovey Dovey was the cake topper who had adorned the top tier of Mrs. B's wedding cake. Her feet had been pressed deeply into its heavy cream cheese frosting, holding her securely in place, though her wings were poised for flight.

Like most toppers, her public life was short and she spent years in a box under Mrs. B's bed. But, eventually, she was taken to the attic. In the process of that transfer, however, the lid to her box got knocked off. And when Mrs. B wasn't looking, Lovey Dovey bolted from her confinement and took to the attic sky, reveling in the freedom of flight, soaring in great loops and glides.

Because of her subsequent aversion to boxes, Lovey Dovey remained a high flier. Yet, every once in a while, at her own will or whim, and nobody could pinpoint why she did what she did, she would swoop down and flutter madly around and just as suddenly leave again. And her visitations always created change which was sometimes appreciated and sometimes not. This day she had flown to the vents and waved in the scent of lilac. And then, with her strong wings, Lovey Dovey whipped gusts of fragrance across the attic and into an eddy that encircled Marmalada Mouse in its perfume.

And as fragrance does, it conjured up old memories for Marmalada Mouse. She remembered being in the kitchen, under the table in a toy basket, when Mr. and Mrs. B were young. Sneaking up behind Mrs. B one spring day while she was doing the dishes, he wrapped an arm around her waist and pulled her close. "Gotcha' some new silk dainties, Kiddo." he whispered. He nuzzled her neck, and brought around a bouquet of sweet pea.

Mrs. B pressed the soft petals against her face. "Oh! My favorite," she sighed, leaning back into his embrace.

Another day he brought in a top-heavy peony that had fallen in the garden. Cradling it in his calloused hand, he presented it to Mrs. B. "Oh, I think this must be my favorite flower," she sighed.

But the deep purple lilac had always been the early bloomer he appreciated most, and when he brought cuttings into the kitchen he asked Mrs. B to put her dishtowel down so that she could give him her full attention. "Now, breathe in," he said, holding the branch under her nose. "Once more," he said, wanting her to get the full impact. "That's the fragrance of new beginnings, Kiddo," he pronounced. And at that moment, of course, lilac was Mrs. B's favorite flower.

Marmalada Mouse brought herself back into the present and inhaled the scent of lilac that was wafting around her, breathing deeply as Mrs. B had done, and letting her back round with each exhale. But within a few minutes her brain shifted into concentration mode and her eyebrows scrunched, the bridge of her nose wrinkled and her eyes darted back and forth, right to left, right to left. Then, all of a sudden, as if she had been stuck with a pin, she snapped to attention.

"The puzzler!" she exclaimed. "Without even trying, I've got it!" Yes, she had half a dozen answers to the first question and she could imagine the same for the others. But there was one answer that would show up for all of them.

What did she like to do, and do well, that no one else did, and that others would pay her to do for them? It couldn't have been more obvious - deliver downstairs news and food. "The answer has been right here, right under my nose," she said to herself, "and I didn't even know it."

Something changed for Marmalada Mouse that day. She had been put in her place, but she had a place to start. And she had a new idea. She would open a downstairs-food store upstairs. But she wisely resisted the impulse to run on blind enthusiasm and decided, instead, to trust Professor Fowler's good advice. So she studied her 7Q Double P, created a preliminary plan, and then with a sense of confidence, made a trip to downstairs.

And it just so happened, that Marmalada Mouse and Mrs. B came down from the attic at the same time.

Marmalada Mouse snuck down behind the wall, while Mrs. B came down the stairs, carrying the tea set for Emerlin and the desk lamp for Big Guy. And while Mrs. B avoided the kitchen that day, Marmalada Mouse raided it, managing to get into a raisin box, the chocolate chip bag, a tin of nuts and a bowl of dry cereal, in addition to the leftover toast and jam bits from that morning's breakfast dishes.

The draped hankies that hid her junk became the backdrop for her new store as Marmalada Mouse carefully laid out her downstairs provisions on blue-checked fabric. People huddled around, anxious to spend their pennies on her tasty treats. Sister Mim crowded in, too, but certainly not to indulge in superfluities. She had a hunch that something was awry and she hoped to expose it. But somebody else took that opportunity away from her.

A whir, a blur and the sound of laughter engulfed Marmalada Mouse again, but without fragrance this time. Instead, Lovey Dovey whipped up an air current sufficient enough to dislodge the carefully draped hankies and send them flying into the air and falling to the floor. Marmalada Mouse's junky junk was thus laid bare for everyone to see.

"How dare you! Why don't you mind your own business?" Marmalada Mouse yelled, shaking a fist at Lovey Dovey. Then, in an attempt to maintain control of the situation, she began hawking snacks, waving them in the air. "Chips, chocolate chips, raisins! Get your snacks here. Half-price snacks!" But she had lost the crowd. Everyone's attention had shifted to her pile of stuff. Remembering how she had been taunted in her nightmare, Marmalada Mouse hung her head and readied herself for ridicule.

But the attic people weren't nightmare meanies. They were her friends and they did their best to make her feel better. "Hey, that's a great belt buckle you've got there," someone called out. "Even though most of the belt has been cut off, it's still got the pokey thing that goes through holes, so it's in operative condition." Others joined in, overacting their approval with exaggerated nods and mm-hmms.

But then there came a predictable "Harrumph!" from none other than Sister Mim, and she insisted on having her say. "Well, I think that Marmalada Mouse has been trying to bamboozle us," she said. With a toothpick in hand, she stepped in closely to probe and jab at stuff as if she had been appointed as some kind of official inspector.

Just then, Benjamin Mojo, a hyperactive musical frog with a shock of red hair, burst into the scene. Benjamin was a "now-you see-him-now-you-don't" kind of a guy who couldn't concentrate, or stay in one place, or sit still for any length of time unless he was making music. He only saw people in his peripheral vision because objects captured the focus of his straight-ahead sight as well as the curiosity of his ears, and he tested the resonance of every item he came across. What may have been a clink, a rattle, a ding, or a clunk to everyone else, was music to him.

"Whatcha' got here Marmalada Mouse?" he asked, bounding past her. And then, like a bee buzzing in a flowery bush, he darted from item to item, tapping for sound. "Nice stuff," he said. But when he touched the hot-red button that was leaning against the "hecho en Mexico" box, he yelped. "Ha-cha-cha! This thing ain't just hot red, its red hot, too!" With that, he was gone.

Sister Mim, wanting to confirm such a phenomenon, stood directly beneath the button, craning her neck to get a good look. But what she saw frightened her. The hot-red button had been dislodged, and it was teetering perilously at the edge of the shelf. "It's going to go!" she cried. And then she ran to save herself.

Her reaction sent others into such a fearful state of ferhoodlement that they began running in circles and into each other. The hot-red button looked like a ball of fire to their frightened eyes as it toppled, landed on edge and began to roll. But then Sister Mim, in a rare, self-forgetful moment of pure motive and some bravery, swung back around and put herself in harm's way. And just as the rolling disk was about to run her down, she leaned hard to the right so that it merely caught the edge of her left foot. That interrupted its course, and to everyone's relief, the hot-red button lost momentum and fell flat to the floor.

Applause erupted and there were hugs all around. However, Sister Mim tried not to be pleased with her own self. She squelched any praise and minimized her heroism, calling it mere duty. So the celebration was cut short, and within a few minutes she was no longer the center of attention. And that bothered her. And the fact that it bothered her bothered her even more because such botheration contradicted her very own point of view. Consequently, she remained cross and bossy.

"Hey, what's goin' on?"

Am I missin' out on somethin?" Bobby Capella asked. He heard the commotion from across the room and came to see what was afoot.

"That is happening!" Marmalada Mouse scolded, pointing to the button on the floor. Then, with angry eyebrows and arms akimbo, she got ready to give him the dickens. But, before she could say a lot of nasty words she would most certainly regret, he quickly responded with a calm voice, his arms folded in front.

"You mean that burner, Marmalada Mouse?" Bobby Capella tipped his head in its direction. "The one like Mrs. B's? You know, the one that keeps the teapot goin' all day? That's the always-on burner that goes on the cute stove I delivered." Then he suggested that he put the appliance together for her, which is something he didn't usually do, but considering the present kerfuffle she might be too upset to figure out how a customized stove like this one went together. And he didn't want to go bragging on himself, but he did mention that he was the one who invented the "custom-i-zation," tch-tch.

Bobby Capella gave Marmalada Mouse an assuring wink and went to work. He hefted the blue, green and black buttons to the stovetop, setting them into the burner holes where they fit as flush as if they had been made for that purpose. Then, using his folded handkerchief as a make-do oven mitt, he picked up the hot-red, red-hot button, and with a "hoo-hah-hah-ouch-ouch," he quickly dropped it into the last burner hole where it snugged in as neatly as the others, and glowed warmly in anticipation of a teapot.

After that, Bobby Capella took the belt buckle and placed the inch of belt that was still attached to it inside the oven, laying it flat on the oven floor. Then he flipped the buckle up against the front of the stove. "That's your closed oven door," he said with some satisfaction, followed by a demonstration of "open and close, open and close," several times.

Then Bobby Capella circled the stove. He noted the rust. "Yeah, tch-tch, she's got patina," he said approvingly. He ran  his hand along one side and down a curved leg, following the highs and lows of the bas-relief scrollwork, a feature that Marmalada Mouse had previously overlooked. "Just look at those flowing lines," he said with admiration. He pondered for a moment and then added, "I don't know for sure, tch-tch, but I think we just might have us an original Art Nouveau here. And you know, Marmalada Mouse, I'd really like to meet that guy because he sure did make one pretty stove!"

Marmalada Mouse cupped her hands over her nose and mouth, barely able to believe her eyes. But she could see that it was indeed a very charming appliance after all. Plus it had to be one-of-a-kind. Nobody else in the whole wide world could possibly have as fine a stove as hers, all flowy and scrolly as it was with big button burners and a buckle oven door!

 Bobby Capella kept going. "Now you can see that this 'hecho en Mexico' box doesn't have its lid, but what it does have are two extra-tall sides that we're gonna' call a headboard and a footboard. Well, let's fill this box with feathers and shreds,

cover them up with a hanky, top that with this doily thing that looks like a fancy fishing net, and plunk down a puffy perfumy thing that looks like a pillow and you've got yourself a bed. Then Bobby Capella proudly pointed out the heavy-duty brads that held the box bed together. "Tch. This thing's built to take a little horseplay. I'd say you've got yourself a genuine customized Mexican jumping bed."

Lastly, Bobby Capella picked up the broken earring. "I know this doesn't look like much," he acknowledged, "since this earring has an empty spot in the middle where a bauble used to be, and the pinchy thing that's supposed to be on the back is missin.'" "But watch this." He laid the earring down, picked up a yellow pencil and stuck the eraser end down into the empty space so that the pencil stood as straight as a telephone pole. Then he sleeved the neck of a perfume funnel onto the pointed lead.

"Easy as that," he said. "You've got yourself a lamp, and nothing less than an authentic Ticonderoga torchier." But as he admired his work, he had to admit that the plastic funnel shade did look a little bachelorish. He turned to Marmalada Mouse and winked again. "I expect you'd probably frilly up that shade with a fancy bit of somethin,' right, Marmsy?"

Marmsy! No one had ever called her that before! But she liked the way it sounded. At least she liked the way it sounded when he said it. She gazed into Bobby Capella's face and something happened in her eyes that made her see for the very first time how very smart and clever and handsome and, yes, how truly honest he truly was. And all of a sudden Marmalada Mouse's heart fluhbubbed so hard it weakened her knees and spurted heat into her cheeks and she couldn't blink.

"Marmsy," Bobby Capella said, looking at her, "I think I'm seeing stars in your eyes, tch-tch."

By the time Bobby Capella was done, he had made sense out of almost everything he had put in her cupboard and he apologized for the few junky things that somehow got included, he didn't know how. "Do you accept my apology, Marmsy?" he asked.

"Oh, I do, I do," Marmalada Mouse assured him. "And do you forgive me for thinking ill of you?" She shook her head in regret. "I should have known."

"I do," he answered happily, "I surely do. In fact I'd say I doo-bee-doo-bee-doo! Tch-tch." Wink.

Bobby Capella and Marmalada Mouse became a team. They pushed the stove out onto the attic floor in front of the cupboard and created a restaurant-kitchen. Then Marmalada Mouse began to work her plan which included daily foraging forays to the main floor. So the attic people settled into a new routine, and downstairs food became regular fare for everyone.

Everyone except Sister Mim. She stayed true to her uppity self, sitting apart at mealtimes, perching stiffly on a hard chair. With eyebrows raised and eyelids held shut in extra-long blinks, she primly nibbled away at her Bakelite fruit plate.

The results of Marmalada Mouse's new discipline were tangible.

Her penny piles were organized and projects were being finished. In spite of that, Marmalada Mouse still struggled against herself, delaying tasks that seemed unfun. So, in an effort to find a way to keep on track she formulated an End-Of-The-Day-Question, her very own and very good EDQ, which was this:

Did I do what I was supposed to do, when I was supposed to do it, whether I felt like it or not?

And once she put those words together Marmalada Mouse was never able to unthink them again. Consequently, she didn't enjoy procrastination much after that, and she grew more and more to be a person of her word, whether she gave it to others or to her own self.

Marmalada Mouse skipped and tra-la-la-ed wherever she went because the future once again seemed promisingly predictable and she expected to live happily ever after. But one dreadful day something awful happened, something she couldn't have foreknown, and something that all of her careful planning could not have prevented. Yet - but unbeknownst to Marmalada Mouse at the time - it is the very kind of thing that happens in an attic world, a rarely visited place, seemingly forgotten and abandoned to the ravages of entropy and enemy alike. And only someone from a bigger world could make it right. Someone from a downstairs world.

A rat commandeered the attic. Gaining furtive entry one morning by gnawing a hole in one of the vents, it crouched like a lion in the grass and wove in and out of the attic streets. Coming upon a meeting being held at the Big Broad Way, the rat stopped in its tracks and dropped to the floor. Only its eyes moved as it sized up the attic people seated in front of him. And after seeing that none of them could match it in size or strength, the bully rat stood to full height in a stance of intimidation.

Bobby Capella had been leading the meeting that day and he was about to ask if there was any old business to attend to when this startling "new business" rose up like a black storm cloud. When his jaw dropped and the color drained from his face everybody knew that he was looking at something terrible, but they were too afraid to turn around to see what it was. Bobby Capella didn't say a word. Grim faced, he just signaled for them to get out of there with a hard jerk of his thumb.

Then with a gruff voice he diverted the rat's attention to himself. "Hey, you!" he yelled. "Yeah, I'm talkin' to you ... you ... you blobby tub o'guts! You awful gob o' spit! What d'ya think you're doin' sneakin' up on people like that?" The rat snorted at such a puny challenge, but instead of plowing right through the chairs to have a go at Bobby Capella, the rat slunk around them, sporting with its prey.

People had caught the meaning of Bobby Capella's gesture, so as the rat was circling, they s-l-o-w-l-y pushed themselves up to a standing position. With knees bent and heads lowered - as if ducking would somehow make them less visible - they stepped to the sides of their chairs, backed up a few steps, and then spun around and scattered like buckshot, looking for the nearest cover each could find.

The rat locked eyes with Bobby Capella and threatened him with a click-ick-ick of its bared teeth. But at that very critical moment, Marmalada Mouse, who had remained by her snack table, acted decisively. She pulled the cover off her treats, released the wheel brake and shoved the table toward the rat, hoping to draw the hulk's attention away from Bobby Capella. Her strategy worked; the rat greedily clutched at the food with both front paws and stuffed its cheeks. Without wasting a second Bobby Capella grabbed Marmalada Mouse by the hand. "Tch. Good work," he said. And off they ran.

Attic life was characterized by dashes for safety after that.

Huge, pushy, crude and rude, there was no taming the rat, and activities cautiously revolved around its unpredictable mood. Sometimes it was preoccupied and left them alone. Some days the rat was just plain lazy and other days, in fits of irritability, it ran roughshod everywhere and over everybody. It might grab any one of them in its jaws and shake that person apart, or shove somebody across the floor with its nose or gnaw off somebody's toes and arms. All manner of evil could befall the person who got careless and encountered the rat. And some of them did.

The Bisque sisters, Jenna Joy and Jubilee, were among them. Everyone agreed, however, that neither of them was to blame for the calamity that had come upon them. They had not been negligent. No, it was not their fault at all.

Jubilee was simply helpless. As an unfinished doll, she lay in a cushioned box where all of her separate parts had been carefully wrapped in tissue, and she was waiting patiently for the day when she would finally be strung together. But the rat destroyed her hopes. It tore into her box and carried off her arms and legs and clothes and hair and scattered them everywhere.

Jenna Joy, a singing-dancing doll with naturally curly hair and as beautiful a dolly as there ever could be, had quite a different experience. She interacted with the rat a number of times, although never at her own initiation. It just so happened – no, it would be more accurate to say that it *seemed to her* that it *just so happened* that they tended to bump into each other.

And when they collided, the rat would gasp with mock surprise and lower its eyes as if to apologize. Then with a diffident grin, a bowed head, a step back and a sweep of a paw that gave her the right of way, it would make room for her to pass by. There was something unsettling about its smile, but the rat had acted rather courtly in her opinion, and on several occasions at that, so she began to think that its reputation as a dirty rotten dastard must have been a gross exaggeration.

Consequently she pushed aside the sense of warning she felt in her stomach when the rat's smile changed from a closed mouth to a show of teeth, and then to a tongue that slowly traced its upper lip from one side to the other. Poor, trusting Jenna Joy, she didn't know she was being toyed with, and when she finally figured it out, it was too late.

At their final encounter, when the rat had tired of its cruel game, there was no courtesy extended at all, just a sudden lurch, a grab and a chomp. The rat expected deliciousness, of course, but a brute appetite can't ever be gratified. No matter how sweet the morsel, it cannot be satisfied. So with a disappointed grimace, the rat spat her out as forcefully as it had clamped down on her.

"Gaak, gaak! Mnyah, mnyah!" the ogre noised, trying to rid its mouth of its own bitterness, but blaming Jenna Joy for it. Who did she think she was to not taste good? Taking revenge with a back-handed whap, the rat knocked the wind and the music right out of her. Then, without a qualm, it lumbered away and Jenna Joy, the beautiful dancing-singing girl, lay on the floor without a note or a step left in her.

True to its nature, the rat continued to prowl. And it was most active at night. So when the sun went down, people had to hide out of reach, and spend their nights in uncomfortably small places. As a result, they often emerged in the morning as tired as they had been the night before. And then, when the rat hailed in a fellow scoundrel to hang out with, some of the citizens gave up altogether and went into hiding permanently.

"I haven't slept for two days and nights," Bobby Capella said.

He put his hand up to stop any comfort Marmalada Mouse might offer because he wasn't looking for sympathy. "And I've noticed somethin'." Pacing, he rubbed his chin and ran his fingers through his hair as if that would help him to think clearly. "I've been watchin' those rats. And there's no where in this attic they don't go … except …" He looked off to the side without finishing his sentence.

"What? Except w-h-a-t?" Marmalada Mouse pleaded impatiently.

"The stove, Marmsy," he said in hushed tones, turning back to look at her. "The rats keep their distance from our stove; they keep their distance from our always-on burner. They know they'll get burned. We've got to put our heads together and figure this thing out."

For several minutes the two of them stood there, forehead to forehead. The pixels in their brains jumped and tumbled and bumped into each other until, like puzzle pieces, they finally found their fit. And when Marmalada Mouse and Bobby Capella stepped apart, each knew what the other was thinking.

"Let's not tell anybody yet," Bobby Capella, said. "Let's just get this show on the road. We've got some arrangin' and customizin' to do."

They filled the floor of the cupboard with as much comfy furniture as they could find, and then shoved the stove up close, positioning it so that only attic-sized people would be able to squeeze by on either side. "Tch-tch, I call this a genuine customized stove-barricade combo, Marmsy," Bobby Capella said with a little hope in his voice. "Let's see if it works."

Darkness came and the attic people raced to their hiding places. The rats stirred, their cavernous mouths agape in yawn, their legs stiffening and claws splaying as they stretched themselves awake. Then, with a flick of the eyelids, and a slap of their long hairless tails, they were ready for their nightly rampage.

When Bobby Capella and Marmalada Mouse heard scratching against the floor, they took their places behind the stove. Afraid, yet determined, they dared the rats to reach past the always-on burner and try to catch them.

It turned out to be a long night, which was good. Time and time again the rats approached, curious at the two small figures refusing to flinch in their presence. And as Bobby Capella had predicted, the rats kept their distance. "They're smart enough to not get burned, Marmsy," he said. "But, I think we might've outsmarted 'em, at least just a little bit. Now, let's get the others to join us."

Marmalada Mouse and Bobby Capella told everybody else about their successful experiment.

But people were used to their own ways of staying safe so it was hard to convince them that they could find protection and company behind the stove. And, as usual, Sister Mim was troublesome. "I think we need to get to the real root of the problem," she said. "And certainly, the importation of downstairs food is what has lured those rats in here." Then Sister Mim got carried away and proposed that Marmalada Mouse, herself, might just be a mini-rat. "Surely, some of you have noticed the similarities, the nose, the whiskers, the snooping around at night, the looting. They loot the attic and she loots downstairs."

Sister Mim's unsettling logic seemed to make some sense, but before any of the others could start pointing fingers, too, Minny Diminuette came to Marmalada Mouse's rescue. "My, oh, my, people," she sighed, "Don't any of you read? We're simply dealing here with the very prevalent rattus rattus."

No, none of them were current on the subject, so Minny Diminuette had to educate them. "The common name for rattus rattus is roof rat," she continued, "and we do live in a roof! None of us is to blame for this. In fact, the sad truth is that it has always been just a matter of time until they overtook us."

Sister Mim's eyes narrowed and her lips tightened. "You have known this all along, and yet you never warned us?" she said through gritted teeth.

"I kept it to myself because you would have lived every day in worry and dread," Minny Diminuette explained, "and we wouldn't have so many good times to remember."

Marmalada Mouse was grateful for Minny Diminuette's defense, and she wanted to hate Sister Mim for her ugly words. But she couldn't, because there was some truth in them. After all, she had gone into Mrs. B's world uninvited. And she had sneakily taken things. And like the rats, she hadn't asked, "May I?" or said "please" or "thank you."

Then again, Marmalada Mouse tried to dismiss any kinship to rats by noting how she differed. In the first place - and this was important to Marmalada Mouse - she was cute. Secondly, she wasn't mean. And thirdly, everything she took was inconsequential. What's an occasional raisin? What's a chocolate chip or two? What's a bit of toast that's headed for the garbage anyway? And what's a … what's a …?
Marmalada Mouse did not want to finish her last question. But she had to: What's a tiara?

Right then and there Marmalada Mouse owned up to the little bit of rat that was in her and she renounced her inner beast. "Sister Mim isn't all wrong," she said, taking the tiara off her head. "This isn't mine to keep. And I must hasten to return it. I'm going to go right now while the rats are still asleep."

"Don't feel too bad, Marmalada Mouse, it doesn't look that good on you, anyway," someone said anonymously.
Marmalada Mouse gasped and she tried to pinpoint the voice in the crowd. But Ella Bouffante stepped forward. "And your tappa-tappa is too loud. Take off your shoes or the rats will wake and chew you to bits."

Marmalada Mouse was about to huff and puff about the talk that had obviously been going on behind her back when Bobby Capella spoke up, insisting that she let him return the tiara for her. But she had to refuse him. "No one else can do it for me," she said. "I'm the only one who knows the wall."

Then Lovey Dovey and Professor Fowler came to the rescue with a promise of protection and direction from the air. "We can see what you can't," they said. "We'll guide you from up here. We'll tell you when to go to the left or to the right or to turn back. And Ella Bouffante is right. You'll have to leave your shoes behind."

"But I have always been able to count on these trusty shoes," Marmalada Mouse protested. "They give me traction when I have to run or climb and stability when I need my balance."

"Well, now you're going to have to trust us," Lovey Dovey said. And so Marmalada Mouse did as she was told. She took off her shoes and set out alone, slipping and sliding in stocking feet.

The attic streets, littered with rodent leavings and cardboard crumbs where the rats had chewed into boxes and pulled stuff out onto the floor, became an obstacle course for Marmalada Mouse to run. Hearing Professor Fowler call "straight ahead," she scrambled up one pile, lost her balance at the top, and rolled down the other side, falling right onto one of the sleeping giants. It raised its ugly head and one huge dark eye opened wide.

Marmalada Mouse thought she was about to be sucked into a black hole right then and there and disappear forever, but then, its eyelid began to close. Slowly, like a garage door, it descended. And when it hit bottom, the rat's head fell back to the floor, its mouth fell open and it resumed its snoring.

Angry and scared, Marmalada Mouse called to Professor Fowler, "Why did you tell me to go straight ahead?"

He swooped to her side. "I didn't say 'straight ahead,' I said 'take a left.' We told you that we would say left, right and back. So, as long as you don't hear from us, whichever way you're facing, just keep on heading that way." Those were hard instructions to trust when straight ahead seemed to come in long stretches and she didn't have the constant comfort of their voices. Nevertheless, their guidance brought her safely to the access corner.

When Marmalada Mouse finally got to the kitchen she saw that the kettle had been taken off the stove and placed on the counter. That told her that Mrs. B was away. So she was able to return the tiara to the jewelry box without hurry. Taking time to peek in every room, she toyed with the idea of never going back to the attic again.

But then she thought of Lovey Dovey and Professor Fowler flying the attic sky to keep her safe, Bobby Capella who had been willing to take her place, Minny Diminuette who had defended her, Tom Purrdy, Ella Bouffante and Pastor Myron - all of them had been friends to her. She had to be a friend to them, too. Besides, she hadn't been invited to come back to Mrs. B's world. So Marmalada Mouse said goodbye forever to downstairs.

Marmalada Mouse was welcomed home with congratulatory hugs.

And Sister Mim hid her disappointment that Marmalada Mouse's repentance had gone so swimmingly. Surely a little more terror, she thought, and even some unforgettable pain would have been more effective in teaching Marmalada Mouse a lesson. But then, Sister Mim felt guilty for having such mean thoughts. And that added to her botheration which now gurgled and roiled inside her like a gassy stomach.

After that, people began to trickle in, taking refuge behind the barricade-stove. Tom Purrdy came after the rats had scattered his penny piles, Ella Bouffante, when the rats messed up her messes and it wasn't easy to find things anymore, and Minny Diminuette, when the rats chewed on her books. Sister Mim held out until she couldn't take lonesomeness any more, which, needless to say, compounded her botheration, because she didn't want to admit that she needed other people. Benjamin Mojo popped in and out on a regular basis, and to everyone's surprise, Lovey Dovey touched down and hung around for a while.

Crammed together with little to do, no place to go, no place to call home, and no hope for the future turned their lives into the worst of times. And yet, there were ways in which they experienced the best of times, too - when they had to have each other's backs, when they moved and worked together as a life-saving team, sharing one heartbeat, and when their favorite word became "remember."

"Talk about downstairs, Marmalada Mouse," someone would say, and she would lean against the stove and sigh, dreamy eyed, and describe each room and recall what happened in them - how artistic creations were born in a dingy furnace room, how childhood heartaches were brought to light in the safety of a dark bedroom, and how important conversations took place in the kitchen, which turned out to be the hub of the house. And the stove. It was the very heart of the hub of the house where communion was prepared - where cocoa was made to warm a body who had come in from the cold, where tea was steeped to welcome the passerby, and where meals put together of ordinary fare made bountiful celebration. She never tired of the telling nor did they of hearing.

Sister Mim spoke up one day to remind them that she was in possession of ordinary fare, ordinary attic fare, that is, her Bakelite fruit plate, which she would be happy to share.

"And I have a clay-bake pie," added Ella Bouffante, her eyes twinkling with self satisfaction. "I hid it from the rats."

Sister Mim's good feelings soured a little when she heard Ella Bouffante's offer. She had seen that pie and it was showier and sweeter than her fruit plate, plus it was super-sized. But she tried to shake her bad feelings, and when they ate together, she almost had the good time that the others actually did.

Mrs. B hurried in from the mailbox to answer the phone.

Emerlin was calling to say she was feeling too sick to pack up the kids and come for dinner. And, yes, Jimmy and Lissa were thrilled to know they were going to have a baby brother. But, no, she wasn't excited about it yet. And, oh, Big Guy did get the new job. However, the medical coverage wouldn't kick in until after the baby was born. And by the way, their lease that was up in two months wasn't going to be renewed so she would have to start looking for a house. Plus, the hot water heater had flooded the utility room and the laundry was piling up - when it rains, it pours, you know. Other than that, she just didn't feel like talking. She would try to call the next day.

Worry kept Mrs. B awake that night. So she got out of bed and went to the living room where the television was on as usual, its volume high enough to alleviate the aloneness of night and overpower noises that could trigger her imagination. Agitated and unable to concentrate, she clicked from channel to channel, eventually tuning in to a telemercial just so she could enjoy hating the kitchen-gadget hawker who ranted at high decibel. "Oh, be quiet," she said after a few minutes, and then turned the television off.

But then the pops and creaks of joints and beams adjusting to the cool of the night unnerved her. And she jumped when the furnace suddenly gunned on. Although she assured herself that these were normal goings on, hoarse scratching sounds, different from the dainty tappa-tappas she had heard on occasion, startled her as she pushed herself forward in the chair. She stiffened as the noise traveled in the walls behind her, up and down, and in the ceiling, across and back. "Rats!" she whispered with grim comprehension, her eyes wide and her mouth turned down as if she had a bad taste in her mouth. Mrs. B snatched her feet off the floor, turned the television back on and curled up protectively under a down throw, finishing the night fitfully in the recliner.

The next day Mrs. B braved the attic after her morning coffee. She opened the hatch slowly, but let it slam to the floor. Then, undoing her belt and pulling it through the loops of her jeans, she clenched her jaw with determination and swung, snapping the buckle end against the floor, whap, clunk, whap. Whooping and whipping, she crisscrossed between boxes, trying not to look down, stomping out a warpath until she felt confident that any and all rats must surely have fled her wrath.

Then Mrs. B calmed down and wandered up and down the cardboard streets examining the ransacked remnants of her past. When she approached the corner cupboard she noticed the crowded toy furniture on the bottom shelf and the tumble of attic people huddled by the stove. Her curiosity was piqued. She stooped to get a closer look, and when she did, something clicked in her head like a first coin dropping into a pop machine. She stood back up and scanned the perimeter of the room. Her eyes stopped at the crib that had been bed for both of her children.

With hands on her hips, Mrs. B looked at the cupboard, then down to the attic people, and over to the crib. She did this several times, and then finally, the second coin dropped. With a snap of her fingers and a "that's it," she went into decisive action. Divesting the cupboard of all its furniture and people, she dragged it back downstairs and put it in Emerlin's old bedroom. She dismantled the crib, too, taking the parts downstairs and leaning them against the bedroom wall.

Then she made several hurried trips back to the attic, whooping and whipping the floor each time she got to the top of the stairs. She gathered up the little furniture, the attic people, fabrics, sheet music, books, strings of Christmas lights, and bits and pieces of miscellany, bending over so many times that her back ached. But she ignored the pain. She was on a mission.

When she had finished her collecting, Mrs. B broke pace for a few minutes and took one last tour of the attic. The sun breaking from behind a cloud revealed a trail of errant ivy that had snuck inside and was creeping across the floor.

"How did you get in here?" She asked. "Max would have a fit if he saw you." She repeated his name, and for a fleeting moment, for the first time in a long time, she was sure she smelled her husband's aftershave, sure she heard his laughter.

She crossed the floor to look at the wall where Mr. B had scribbled preliminary plans for the bedrooms that never got built. Running her fingers over the black marks, she said goodbye again to what had been and what would never be. Then Mrs. B headed for the stairs. She needed to call Big Guy and ask him to set some traps.

Emerlin's old bedroom became a temporary craft room.

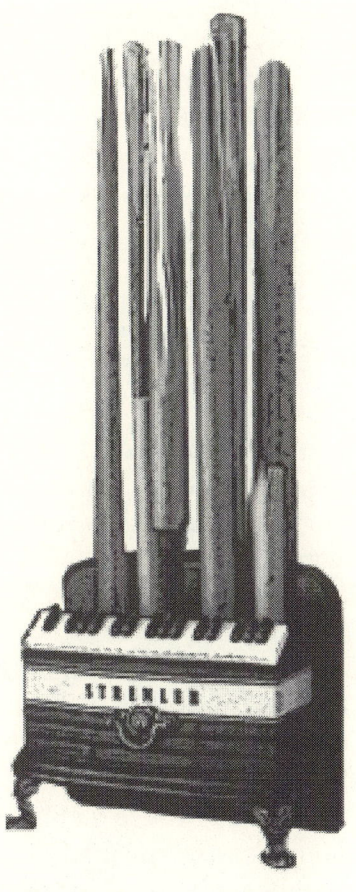

Mrs. B made a work surface out of a piece of plywood, bridging two vanity drawer stands that flanked a center mirror. Tools and supplies came up from the furnace room, and then Mrs. B went to work. First, she chose fabric remnants that would become floor coverings and wallpaper for a living room at the base of the cupboard, a kitchen on the first shelf, a library on the second, and a bedroom on the third. She designated the top shelf as a music room and papered its walls and ceiling with sheet music, choosing one song to feature prominently - "Amazing Grace" - which she believed was both appropriate and beloved enough to be an alternate National Anthem.

Then Mrs. B furnished the house, beginning at the top. The music room with its high ceiling called out for special treatment, which meant that an ordinary piano, even if it were a grand, would not suffice. So she invented a wind chime pipe organ. A curved, dark wooden box standing on brass feet became its console, onto which she affixed at the front a keyboard taken from a broken toy, and above which she suspended as its pipes a double set of wind chimes that had once hung outside her kitchen door. She rubbed furniture polish into the dark wood and noted the brand name on the box. "Stremler - that's a good name for a pipe organ," she said to herself. "Its sound is both musical and strong." So she was careful to leave it intact.

Mrs. B took satisfaction in her work, and she wondered what life was like for children who didn't make things anymore, whose toys came to them from the store so fully ideated by adult minds that there was nothing left to do except to move them around a bit. She was convinced that some part of many young brains was being sorely neglected.

After several hours each room had been supplied with decorations and paintings and bouquets and furniture arrangements, so Mrs. B attended to the most important aspect of any house - putting people in it.

Everybody needed some tidying up before they got placed, but Mrs. B took extra time with Marmalada Mouse. "However you managed to show up in my kitchen one day and disappear again, I'll never know," she said, "but whatever you're doing, it's ruining your clothes."

Mrs. B constructed a new dress for Marmalada Mouse from an outdated black silk blouse. She stitched a double vertical row of tiny gold buttons onto the fitted bodice running them from the waist to the white stand-up collar that curled under Marmalada Mouse's chin. The long sleeves that puffed at the shoulder were finished at the wrist in a dangle of white lace. And the gathered skirt, trimmed with gold beads, came all the way to the floor.

Holding Marmalada Mouse at arm's length, Mrs. B said, "You almost look like royalty. Perhaps you should have a crown of some sort." She fingered through her sewing notions unsuccessfully and then noted the plain slender ring, thin and bent with age that loosely fit her own finger. "This seems appropriate," she said, securing it to Marmalada Mouse's head with a fine thread. Satisfied with her choices Mrs. B stopped there. Pressing down on her work surface, she got to her feet with a groan. She rolled her head around slowly several times and rubbed the small of her back. Then she went to the kitchen to figure out a late dinner and put in a call to Sterling.

Marmalada Mouse spun around to look in the mirror, eager to revel in her queenly image. But she was disappointed in garb that seemed rather plain for royalty. Where were the rings and brooches and strands of pearls? And weren't crowns supposed to be adazzle with jewels? And surely a queen should have natural curls! But Marmalada Mouse wasn't in a position to make demands, so she lowered her standards and came to terms with the reflection in the mirror and practiced waving to loyal subjects.

Something told Mrs. B that Marmalada Mouse was not quite finished.

She returned to her project and snipped loose threads from Marmalada Mouse's gown, and stitched a pearl to the collar, which didn't add much to the overall effect. Then she set her aside, sat back in her chair and just looked at her for a while.

Marmalada Mouse assumed that a new project was in process when Mrs. B finally began cutting up an old pillowcase and talking to herself about making a pinafore. But she was mistaken. It was being made for her.

Mrs. B starched and ironed the tiny pinafore and slipped it over Marmalada Mouse's new dress, securing its ties in a big bow. It was a long over-garment, leaving just a slim border of dress visible at the bottom. A ruffle on both sides of the bib ran up from the waist, over the shoulders and down to the tie in back.

But that wasn't the end of Mrs. B's modifications. She also looped a ribbon around the front of the gold ring on Marmalada Mouse's head, twisting it into a rosette and a bow that hid the modest crown. Then she turned up the white lace at Marmalada Mouse's wrists to create simple cuffs and turned her stand-up collar down. Finally, she pinned a gold key to the waistband of the pinafore.

When Marmalada Mouse managed to sneak another peek in the mirror, she saw that her crown had been eclipsed by the bow, her collar and cuffs were plain, and most of her dress was covered up. "Pinafore is just a fancy word for apron," she said dejectedly. "I'm wearing a uniform. I am a maid."

But Mrs. B was happy with what she had done. She placed Marmalada Mouse in her cupboard-house kitchen, facing outward with her arms extended as if she were ready to greet guests with a big hug.

"Now, as for you, Queen Mouse," she said instructively, "There are two things you must never forget," She tapped a fingernail against Marmalada Mouse's crown - tappa-tappa.

"Number One: Remember who you are behind that bow and underneath that pinafore.

"Number Two - and every genuine royal knows this to be true - Remember this:

"She who would be great must be the servant of all."

With that, Mrs. B walked to the doorway and turned off the bedroom light. Silhouetted there by light from the hall, she looked back, her hand still on the switch, and said, "The best to ever come into this world said that, you know."

Then she padded to her own bedroom, her feet swollen from sitting so long. She fell asleep that night with her legs propped up on a pillow.

Emerlin and the children accompanied Big Guy when he came to set traps for Mrs. B.

They brought take-out dinner with them, pizza, salad, garlic sticks and drinks. Unloading everything in the dining room, they ate at the unset table, poking their plastic forks into the boxed salad and using paper towels for pizza plates.

"I'm going to Montana," Mrs. B said while they were eating, "and I won't be back until Christmas." Emerlin and Big Guy were too surprised to comment. "I'm going because I need your help," she added.

"I don't get it, Mom," Emerlin said.

"Em, honey," she answered, putting her fork down and leaning on her elbows. "Shortly after Sterling and Angie remodeled their house, they fixed a room up especially for me and I've never taken them up on their offer to come and stay for a while. Plus, this house of mine is falling apart, and I've lost the heart to fix it. If you and Big Guy and the kids could move in for a while, you could finish out the bedrooms in the attic and make repairs in exchange for rent. It could be a win-win situation for all of us. Just think, you wouldn't have the stress of finding a new place, the kids could have their own rooms upstairs, and they could walk to school."

Mrs. B reasoned on, pushing hard to have her way. And she didn't want them to say they would go home and think about it, so she told them she already had a bus ticket. She was scheduled to leave in two weeks. "Is it a deal?" she finally asked. It was a deal. "Good," she said triumphantly, slapping both hands on the table. "Now come and look. I've given you a head start on the baby's room."

Everybody trailed to Emerlin's old bedroom. "A doll house?" asked Big Guy when he spotted the corner cupboard, "In a boy's bedroom?"

"Actually," Mrs. B answered. "I think that could be classified as an action figure house."

Action figure! At that, Jimmy did a double take and moved in for a closer look. "Gramma doesn't know the definition of action figure," he thought to himself. But he didn't correct her because he liked what he saw and he wanted to be able to say so. "Yeah, it looks like everybody in here is doing somethin'," he said casually. "Besides, dad, you work on houses. Is there some rule that says you can only work on full-size ones?" Big Guy conceded the point.

They all found something to appreciate in Mrs. B's work and started to come up with ideas for their own contributions. Then Emerlin noticed two small boxes still on the vanity, clearly marked, as Mrs. B's boxes always were. One said, 'Repair,' the other, 'Finish.' "And what's in the boxes, Mom?" she asked.

"Oh, I felt like taking some handwork with me," Mrs. B answered. She took off the lids and revealed Jenna Joy, the worn-down dancing girl felled by the rat, and Jubilee, whose scattered parts Mrs. B had retrieved.

"This little dancing girl is one of the prettiest dolls I ever made, so I think she warrants repair," she said of Jenna Joy. "And this other one never got finished," she said, putting the lids back on the boxes. "And as you know, it bolsters a person's sense of self respect to complete a project." Mrs. B rolled her eyes at herself and added, "No matter how long it takes."

It was time to go, but Mrs. B had to make one more nervous trip to the bathroom.

She brushed her hand along the living room wall as she went by. "Now you'll have more to listen to than one old lady talking to herself," she said. "Take good care of my girl."

She had refused to let them drive her to the bus station, so Big Guy loaded her bags into a cab and he and Emerlin and the children said goodbye from the edge of the driveway, all of them a little misty-eyed. Mrs. B waved from the rear window until the cab crested the rise in the road.

And then, without warning, she fell apart, sobbing audibly. Was she dreading change that much, she wondered? Feeling loss? Hating the word goodbye? Crying old tears? Whatever it was made her sick to her stomach. Breathing deeply and deliberately with her hands pressed against her stomach didn't quell her nausea, so she gestured frantically to the driver to stop. But he had already noticed her distress and was pulling over to the side of the road.

Bolting from the back seat, Mrs. B staggered blindly onto the parking strip. She bent over and retched several times, clinging, she thought, to the sleeve of the driver who was kind enough to stand by her. She would be sure to thank him for his kindness with a generous tip. But as her vision cleared, Mrs. B could see that she had lost that morning's coffee and toast not just on the grass but on somebody's socks and shoes, too. Somebody's squeaky shoes. Somebody's huaraches. The handsome man who often walked by her house had seen her stumble out of the car and it was he who had rushed to her side.

Mrs. B wished that she could disappear. Humiliation engulfed her. Plus, she knew what she looked like when she cried. And it wasn't like movie stars whose tears glistened like diamonds in their eyes, enhancing their beauty. No, her face and neck would be blotchy, her eyes red and swollen, her mascara smeared and her nose blocked so that her ems and ens would sound like bees and dees.

But she couldn't stay crouched forever. She had a bus to catch. So, she straightened up, looking at the man's shirt, avoiding his face. "Thak you," she said, "I'b ... I'b odd by way to Bodtada. By sud lives there."

"Well, I hope you're coming back," the gentleman said, handing her a handkerchief from his pocket.

"Oh, thak you again," she said, "Yes, I'll be hobe for Chrissbas. I'b just getteeg out of the way while by daughter and sud-id-law bake sub repairs odd by house."

"We haven't formally met," he said. "My name is Philip Johnson. My friends call me Phillie."

"Well, how do you do, Philip?" She wiped her face with a tissue stashed in her sleeve rather than dirtying his handkerchief.

"Phillie," he countered.

"Phillie," she answered, lifting her face. When she braved eye contact, a current of ease passed between them so naturally that it didn't even take Mrs. B by surprise. It was as if they had been friends for a very long time and were picking up where they last left off. Mrs. B's nose cleared, enabling her to speak normally again. "My name is Frances, Frances Burjanavetti," she said." He cocked his head and raised his eyebrows in surprise at her last name. "My friends call me Frances B," she joked.

"I was a contractor in my day," he informed her. "If you think your son-in-law might need a tip or two I could stop by."

"Oh, no thank you," Mrs. B said. "He is quite capable." But in a nanosecond she reconsidered her words and quickly added, "However, as they say, two heads are better than one." (How she came up with such a trite expression, she did not know.) "My daughter Emerlin will be happy to make you a cup," she said. "Her husband is Big Guy. And he is a big guy, so watch out for his handshake."

"Okay, then," Mr. Johnson said. "But I think I'll buy a new pair of shoes first." He waited for her reaction.

"Good idea," she said. "Perhaps you could look for some real ones." He appreciated the sarcasm.

The cab driver checked his watch and interrupted their conversation with a tap on the horn. "You ready yet, lady?" he called.

"Yes, I'm ready," she answered. Mr. Johnson handled the passenger door for her and the driver headed into traffic again.

Mrs. B riffled through her purse and found her compact. She opened it and glanced at herself in the small round mirror, and snapped it shut. She looked worse than she had imagined. So, she pulled out her sunglasses and put them on and rolled the window down to get some fresh air in her face. She relaxed and let the wind play with her hair.

Sounds of the city whizzed by - a motorcycle, a siren, a horn, a jackhammer. But it was a little voice that caught her attention, a voice she hadn't actually heard yet. It was the voice of a little boy soon to be born who would surely come into this world, like his brother before him, with an innate appreciation for the baser things of life. Mrs. B could hear his delight. "Gramma, tell me about the time you threw up all over Grampa Phillie's shoes."

Gratitude was the prevailing attitude in the corner cupboard house.

Its tiny people were back where they belonged. They were home. Doubly so, actually, in the little house made suitably and especially for them inside a bigger house they could also call their own again, and they relished downstairs life.

As Christmas neared and activity increased, they hoorayed when Sterling and Angie brought Mrs. B home from Montana. They felt the air cool when the front door was held open for Big Guy as he struggled to get the Christmas tree into the living room. They heard "shushes" and giggling when presents were snuck into hiding places. They listened in on friends and neighbors who dropped by for eggnog. And they endured the suspenseful quiet when the whole family rushed out of the house one night because the new baby was coming.

Brendon James James was a big baby, nine pounds of robust health. He had wisps of corn silk hair and his cheeky face seemed wider than it was long. He was an easy baby, sleeping contentedly most of the time, and when he wasn't sleeping, somebody was kissing him. He slept in a bassinette in his parents' bedroom for his first week, but on Christmas Eve they decided to let him try out his crib.

It took the whole family to put him to bed. Lissa and Jimmy lined up his stuffed animals. Mrs. B stood ready with his quilt as Emerlin secured him on his side between supportive pillows. Big Guy adjusted the mobile above his head and switched on the nightlight. Sterling and Angie watched from the doorway. When Brendon settled in without complaint, Big Guy herded everyone out of the room, leaving the door slightly ajar. "Oops, forgot something," he said. Leaning on the knob as he swung the door back open, he addressed the cupboard people in a loud whisper. "Don't you guys keep our boy awake, now."

Marmalada Mouse gazed at the tiny mound of quilt in the crib across the room.

And for the first time in all the months she had been contentedly ensconced as the lady of her house, she saw a reason to venture outside of it. But she held back, afraid to trespass, to overstep, to disrespect the generosity of Mrs. B, who, while accomplishing her own purposes, had also managed to restore Marmalada Mouse's cherished dreams. She threw her arms into the air in frustration, but when they dropped to her sides again, her left arm brushed against the key that had been pinned to her pinafore. "The key!" she cried, clutching at it so hard she almost tore her apron. "Mrs. B gave me a key!"

Perplexed, Marmalada Mouse raised one eyebrow and rubbed her chin. "A person uses a key to get inside a house." she mumbled to herself. "But I'm already in." Then, twirling the key clockwise and counterclockwise and back again, she pondered what to do. She tried to account for the fact that the cupboard house didn't actually have any doors, and therefore no locks and consequently no keyholes. "The key must be a symbol," she concluded, "a symbol of freedom, freedom to come and go."

Then Marmalada Mouse thought about her crown. It was a symbol, too, of royalty, even though it was hidden behind the bow on her head. And since queens are free to do what they want to do, why would she need the key at all? Then it dawned on her that Mrs. B had not attached the key to her queenly gown, she had pinned it to her maidly apron, and maids have work to do.

"Responsibility and freedom," she concluded, "they must go together." But Marmalada Mouse could not imagine anything irresponsible about wanting to see a baby. So, without any more deliberation, she slipped from her kitchen down to her living room and out onto the bedroom floor.

"Oh, no!" her friends cried. "There goes Marmalada Mouse again! And our peace and quiet!" But most of them really shared her excitement.

Marmalada Mouse got just half way across the room when Brendon began to cry. "Quick," she called back, "Somebody, do something! Somebody sing a lullaby!"

Sister Mim, prone as she was to respond to emergencies, was the first to heed the call.

But lacking a lullaby in her repertoire, she referred to the music on the wall. With eyebrows aslant and her chin tucked in toward her neck, Sister Mim began, "A-may-ay-ay-ay-ay-zi-ing gray-ay-ay-ace." It sounded as if chocolate were stuck in her throat, and her vibrato wobbled unsteadily, obscuring the melody. But Sister Mim thought this moment was meant for her and she for the moment, not only for the baby's sake but for the other people in the cupboard as well, and one in particular, Marmalada Mouse, whom she hoped was listening very carefully to the words of the song.

In spite of Sister Mim's warbling, however, or perhaps because of it, the baby cried louder. But she sang on. And just as she approached the phrase, "that saved a wretch like me," something inside her popped. The strain of suppressing botheration for so long had finally brought her inner censor to the point of fatigue and it had blown. Consequently, she pointed at Marmalada Mouse, unable to hide her resentment any longer, and sang, "That saved a rat like you."

And then suddenly, the room was filled with a familiar whir, a blur, and the sound of laughter, and time screeched to a halt. Everybody froze, mid-step, mid-gesture, and mid-word. Everybody but Sister Mim. For her, the still silence was shattered by the sound of a sonic boom. She looked up with dread and saw a sky, and in that sky, a javelin zooming through a cloud. Momentarily encouraged, she thought it might be the magic wand of her wishes, so she lifted her hands to receive the muddy brown trim she had coveted for so long. At last, she would be two-toned.

But the javelin contorted above her, zigzagging like lightning and snapping loudly across the blue like a belt against an attic floor. Then it transmogrified into an arrow of blame that swung around and pointed directly at her, pulsing its accusation. A third time it changed, curling into a fist with an extended index finger that wagged shame at her. "No, no," Sister Mim whimpered. "You've got the wrong person."

Then the fist disintegrated into a million shreds that came back together again, entwined into a lasso that looped right into Sister Mim's inside self and yanked it out. She was slated for an out-of-body experience. Standing there, gawking at a seeming stranger who had botheration in her furrowed brow, botheration in her haughty glare, in the down-turned corners of her mouth, and in her stiff neck, she mumbled, "That person doesn't look very happy." But when she said "that person," she really knew she should have said "I" because from head to toe the figure was telltale white.

The words were hardly out of her mouth, however, when the lasso yanked her back into herself for an in-of-body experience that showed Sister Mim her inner stuff. She recoiled when she saw that her shriveled heart, gone pale as her skin and past repair, had been replaced by a botheration machine that pumped its poison everywhere. She wanted desperately to flee, but the lasso wrapped itself tightly around her knees and held her fast until at last she cried, "Yes, I am looking at me." With that, the lasso fell to the floor.

At Sister Mim's moment of truth, Lovey Dovey flew out of the room. And in a fit of flurrious flappage, she swooped through the house and rounded up all the holiday aromas - turkey, pumpkin pie, cranberry muffins, hot apple cider, cinnamon candles, pine bows, and the fir tree. So powerful were her wings that even the essence of Christmases past followed her back to the nursery and into the cupboard where they swirled around Sister Mim, baptizing her in a tide of perfume, and she had no choice but to breathe it in. Breath upon breath, Sister Mim absorbed the aromas of that Christmas Eve day along with redolence from the dusty roads of long ago and far away. Cinnamon and pine and fir mingled with hay and frankincense and myrrh.

Infused with the fragrance of an ancient beginning deeper and older than memory, Sister Mim began to understand the writing on the wall. That song was her song. Hers, because she was the wretch. Jealous, critical and self-righteous, she snooped out other people's misdeeds instead of her own. "What may be wrong with Marmalada Mouse is wrong with me," she admitted to herself. "What's wrong with the world is wrong with me."

Immediately, the lasso at her feet leapt into the air and transformed once more coming at her this time like a branding iron that had been held in the fire. It slammed into her chest and could have knocked her down, but Sister Mim stayed on her feet and took the hot pain. "I wanted Marmalada Mouse to suffer," she said to herself. "Now I guess it's my turn."

Then in a flash, time resumed its regular pace and no one knew what Sister Mim had endured. She nervously cleared her throat and asked to start her song again.

"Amazing Grace," She began tentatively.

"How sweet the sound." Her voice steadied.

"That saved a wretch …" She paused an eighth's beat time, inhaled audibly, and then let loose.

"Like ME-E-E!"

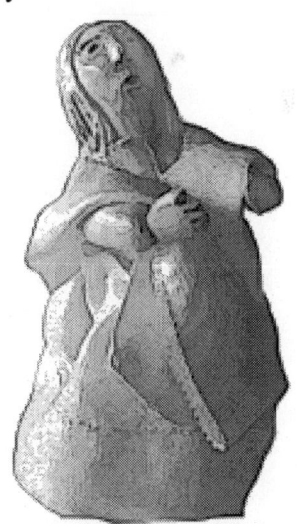

She hit that D above high C to a T, and she held it long and her voice was strong because she sang the truth.

And hearing that note above his own cry, baby Brendon began to settle down. So Sister Mim could have sung on, but she was shaken by her experience and she needed to think about things, so she ceded the floor to Bobby Capella.

Ella Bouffante rushed to her side. "Thank you for singing," she said, "You've never shown such heart before."

Sister Mim accepted the compliment, putting a hand on her chest where the iron had seared her, the place were a heart should be. But something felt strange to her touch and oddly warm. She looked down to see what was different.

And there, to her amazement, was her desire come true - a second color. And it wasn't a humble muddy brown or just a band on her sleeves. It was a big conspicuous hot-red, red-hot heart bursting from the inside out.

Chirpy as a child with new shoes, Sister Mim could hardly take her eyes off her new heart.

But upon careful examination, she found that she had been given much more than color. Firmly embedded in it, identifying her heart as genuine, authentic and true, was an Ever Steady Ready Empathizer, the power source that now enabled Sister Mim to care for other people, to understand their hopes and dreams and fears and pain, and not just her own.

However, that in turn generated an unavoidable feeling of sadness for her former hurtful ways. And that, in turn again, destroyed the joy of the moment and made her want to run away from herself and hide from everybody else, too. So she backed away from the singing. And when she came up against the wall, she slowly slid to the floor and crouched there, clutching her legs to her chest, and dropping her forehead heavily onto her knees.

But Pastor Myron was on the alert, and he noticed Sister Mim off by herself. So he sidled in her direction and cleared his throat to get her attention. She looked up at him with her hands against her cheeks, her eyes wide and her mouth agape as if she were encountering a frightful sight. "Oh, I have been so hateful, so mean, so nasty, so selfish," she cried. Then she grabbed hold of her legs again and hung her head.

Pastor Myron comforted her with a timid pat on the shoulder and launched into a question and answer exhortative monologue. "Your repentance is good and proper, Sister Mim, but we don't want to get fixated on how bad we are, now do we?" He shook his head, as she did hers without looking up. "No, certainly not," he continued, "That's just another way of being self-absorbed, isn't it?" They both nodded.

"And, if you read the writing on the wall," he said, gesturing toward the sheet music above them, "You will see an adjective up there, won't you? Yes you will. And which word is the adjective? Yes, it is the word 'amazing.' And what noun is that adjective modifying? Ex-a-a-ctly," he said, dragging the word out, and pointing to her approvingly as if she had come up with the right answer even though she hadn't said a thing.

"Yes," he cheered. "It modifies the word 'grace.' *That* is what is amazing! So, we wouldn't want to lose our way by focusing on errors that simply fizzle in comparison, now would we?"

Zzt. A little spark went off in Sister Mim's new heart.

Pastor Myron's brain was abuzz with profundity and he couldn't hold his thoughts to himself. "And, consider this, Sister Mim," he said as the idea came to him, "We're all the same, you know. We just take turns failing each other. Some days we do the right thing and some days we don't."

Zzt. Another spark.

As Pastor Myron rambled on, sparks piled up on each other until at last they ignited a surge of truth that jumpstarted a new and true kind of confidence in Sister Mim. So, like a butterfly freed from its cocoon, she was able to relax her furrowed brow, release her frown and let go of the hold she had on herself. She jumped to her feet with open arms and a smile on her face.

Pastor Myron readied himself for an appropriate pastoral hug, anticipating her usual chill. But an unusual sense of warmth took him by such surprise that he stepped back. It was then that he noticed something he had failed to fully appreciate before. "Sister Mim! That's quite a heart you have there!" he gulped.

"Yes," Sister Mim responded, taking control of their conversation at last. She linked her arm in his. "Let me tell you how I got it."

Bobby Capella had taken the floor at Sister Mim's invitation.

He beckoned for antsy Benjamin Mojo, the hyperactive musical frog who had been pacing impatiently, waiting for a chance to pounce on the wind chime organ. Benjamin sprang readily to the mighty Stremler. But he fidgeted on the bench so long it seemed as if he would never actually play. He straightened his tie, ran his fingers through his hair, measured his reach to the keyboard, adjusted his position to get a fraction of an inch closer, changed his mind and scooted back again, returned to his tie and hair and checked his reach again.

Finally, he thrust his arms high in the air, arching his fingers, ready for attack. Then down they came, and in a dizzying display of flying spatulate fingers and toes Benjamin Mojo made the Stremler's chimes ring out in veritable angel song, celestial scales broad and long and deep and high that filled the air and stilled it at the same time, and hushed his audience.

When Bobby Capella broke the silence, he spoke reverently. "Maestro Mojo on the pipes, ladies and gentlemen," he said. Then, with a nod and a sideways glance he directed Benjamin Mojo into a ballad. "Mary had a baby," he crooned, loosening his bow tie, "Oh-oh, yeah." Ella Bouffante joined him, lifting her trunk and trumpeting a soft wah-wah counterpoint. "And our very own Ella Bouffante on the horn, tch," he said.

Then with a wink he signaled Benjamin Mojo to pick up the pace so that the broken dollies Mrs. B had made brand new again could make their debut. There they were - Jubilee with her feet under her at last, and Jenna Joy, as beautiful as before and fully restored. Catching their groove together, the two of them rode the rhythm of the Stremler with fan kicks, calypso leaps, floats and freezes, and the electric slide.

People cheered. Their feet started tapping. Hands were clapping and in the air. Everybody sang. In an out of tune. It didn't matter. Even the walls purred in response to melodic molecules jostling across the room.

But such exuberance made Pastor Myron uneasy. (He was Presbyterian.) Stepping in view of the dancers with concerned eyebrows and arms held out as if to stop traffic, he tried to moderate their behavior and suppress the accelerating crescendo with a corrective glare. When that didn't work, he turned to the crowd, searching for eye contact. But it was futile. They would have none of it. There was Joy to the World in that cupboard. And it would not, could not be suppressed.

Mrs. B was glad to be home for the holidays.

It was a season filled with family tradition. Although presents weren't exchanged until Christmas morning, Lissa and Jimmy got to open their gifts from Uncle Sterling and Aunt Angie after dinner on Christmas Eve. Then at nine thirty, Mrs. B served the children cocoa topped with marshmallows which they drank in the living room in front of the fireplace. And just before their ten o'clock bedtime, a glass of milk and a snicker doodle were set out for Santa.

After Lissa and Jimmy were tucked in, the adults gathered in the living room with a hot pitcher of coffee nudge. They turned up the Christmas music and listened with minimal conversation. Big Guy was the first to notice when the clock read past midnight. "It's Christmas," he said. He went over to Santa's snack and bit off a substantial bite of cookie and gulped down half the milk. Then he took Emerlin's hand and pulled her up from the couch. "See you in the morning," they said. Sterling and Angie chatted with Mrs. B for a few more minutes and then turned the music down for her and said their goodnights, too, leaving her alone in the living room.

Mrs. B was always the last to go to bed on Christmas Eve. That was when she attended to her final Christmas Eve ritual. Pulling a gift bag from underneath the Christmas tree, she removed the tissue at the top and brought out the Nativity Child in his shoebox manger. He had been part of their Christmas tradition since Emerlin was six years old and Sterling, four. It had been their gift to her, a shoebox stuffed with wads of Kleenex bearing a nondescript fabric doll with a worn face, pulled from their toy box. It was swaddled in a pink washcloth held in place by an awkward tie of blue rickrack. A yellow pipe cleaner halo fit his head like a loose sweat band.

Mrs. B had been taken aback by his homeliness and had to manufacture happy surprise when they presented this

Christmas babe to her. She had been looking to find a doll herself that year but hadn't found one to her liking, and she must have said so in the children's hearing. She had envisioned a bright eyed doll with pink cheeks, however, and a vintage basket for his bed, crimped brown paper confetti strips mixed with metallic gold threads for hay, back lighting around his head and a patchwork quilt made of pieced jewel-tone fabrics.

For surely Mary, herself, as humble as her circumstances must have been, surely she had prepared something special for the Son of God. But as for the baby Mrs. B then held in her hands, there was no way to tactfully fix him up to make him go with her carefully executed Christmas décor. And she knew she was stuck with him.

But when she looked up to say an artificial thank you, the sight of her children's beaming faces brought her to her senses. They had done the very thing she appreciated so much, taken resources at hand and made something of them. And they had made that something for her. And there they were, standing before her, grinning with so much pride and anticipation and love that when she looked down at their humble offering again, she saw it with new eyes. And the plain baby Jesus simply stole her heart. "Oh, he's just what I needed," she was able to say. "I will keep him forever."

So Mrs. B did what she had done every Christmas Eve since then. She gave the shoebox baby his place of honor at the center of the raised hearth. Mrs. B knelt in front of him, leaning her arms on the warm stone, and turned her gaze to the Christmas tree flanking the fireplace. Hypnotized by the lights that danced in her eyes, she sang along with her favorite Christmas carol in a lethargic intermittent whisper, sometimes just mouthing the words, "Oh, little town … how still … yet in thy dark streets … everlasting light … The hopes and fears of all the years are met in thee tonight."

Then the sound of the word "Gramma" broke her reverie. Startled, she turned to see Jimmy and Lissa standing by the couch. "We can't sleep," they said in unison.

"Neither can I," she answered. "Go get your pillows and blankets, but do it quietly. Let's not wake anybody else up."

The children scooted down the hall and returned to the living room, pillows in hand, dragging their blankets behind them. They set up camp for the night on the floor in front of the fireplace while Mrs. B added a couple of logs to the fire. Then she curled up on the couch behind them, covering herself with a throw and wedging an accent pillow under her neck.

"Gramma," Jimmy said, "tell us about Christmas when you were a kid."

Marmalada Mouse reached Brendon's crib as the last Christmas carol cast its slumberous spell on the household.

The soft murmur of conversation in the living room ceased as Lissa and Jimmy succumbed to sleep in spite of their excitement. The fire dwindled to embers.

On his side, Brendon lay with one cheek flattened against a flannel sheet that absorbed his drool. Dreaming, his eyes darted back and forth behind closed lids. His mouth twitched a flicker of a smile. Fearing that he might wake and cry out, Marmalada Mouse held her index finger against her lips, signaling the cupboard people to hush as she cautiously crept toward him.

But he didn't rouse. His sleep was sound. Then, as if he were almost too fragile to touch, she gently pressed her whiskered cheek against his downy head and patted the dimpled knuckles of his chubby hand. Hungry-eyed, she tried to memorize every detail, clinging to the moment as if somehow by trying she could make it last longer than a moment can.

Aflutter with excitement, she knelt beside him with folded hands, her posture a prayer. Her heart was in her eyes as she peered into his baby face, hoping to catch a flash of transformation. And that anticipation settled her down. Content in the still and dim, Marmalada Mouse watched him while he slept, and breathed the rhythm of his breath.

Made in the USA
Charleston, SC
14 October 2010